Stone Thrower

Also by Mike Casper
The Sing Song Child

Stone Thrower

Mike Casper

Sing Song Publishing

First Edition

Published in the United States of America by Sing Song Publishing®

978-0-9905144-1-1 (paperback)
978-0-9905144-2-8 (eBook)

Cover design: Jesica Rogus
Interior artwork: Heather Miller

Biblical reference and quotes: Zondervan NIV Study Bible, 1985.

This is a work of fiction. Characters appearing in this work are based
upon actual historical characters mentioned in the *Holy Bible,* with
the sole exception of the old soldier in 'Golden B Flat Cinnamon' who
is merely a product of the author's imagination.

There is no better excuse for strengthening the heart, than to reach down and lift another up.

—Anonymous.

Contents

Preface

I'd always wondered about the man with the withered hand. He lived, and Jesus healed him. That's it. But what was his life before the miracle? And, after he was made whole, what did he do?

I named him 'Achim' and wrote *Bread, Beer, and Rabbit Lentil Stew to* tell his story. It seemed only natural that I continue with *Centurion.* After all, not much is known about him either. One story always led to the next, eventually totaling fifteen, about real people briefly mentioned in one or more of the Gospels of Matthew, Mark, Luke, and John. These folks had an encounter with Jesus of Nazareth. Then they faded away, lost in the swirling sands of time.

Not anymore.

Bread, Beer, and Rabbit Lentil Stew

I think it was my withered hand that drew his sympathy. That useless, wasted thing had always defined my life. Indeed, it has for all of us deformed people.

But especially me.

I hated my hand. Sure, I hid it well with my easygoing, jovial demeanor, but somehow Jesus saw the bitterness, pain, and despair deep in my heart. How I don't know.

But it touched him.

When I was very young, my father said I mustn't limit myself, that there was nothing I couldn't do. There was never any room for self-pity. He'd say, "Achim, focus on what you can do," which to him, of course, was everything. And, while one of my hands was withered, the other was not, a fact overlooked by bullies. Eventually, they learned to leave me alone.

My father also tasked me with developing my intellect and my sense of humor. I learned to speak, read, and write, Greek, Latin, Hebrew, and Coptic Egyptian. Wisdom indeed.

I became a woodworker, of all things, eventually rising to the position of Master Craftsman. I was the best of the best—not bad for a guy with a withered hand.

I opened a shop, and for a while, I had more business than I could handle. Then, for some reason, people quietly stopped buying my goods. After a few months I found out that a very prominent Pharisee had wondered aloud in the temple if my withered hand was a curse from God—and if by having my chairs and tables in their homes, people would be inviting affliction and sin in as well.

Who should the people believe? The temple's authority or a man with a withered hand? I sure didn't feel cursed, but position almost always trumps truth. For the short term anyway.

What the priest didn't say was that I'd refused to make a secret portal into his concubine's home next door. Wasn't adultery wrong for priests *and* ordinary citizens? Because of my refusal, he'd been afraid I'd publicly expose him to the temple, despite my assurances that his intentions were between him and God.

That wasn't enough. To cover his treachery, the priest swore to destroy me. And he did.

I lost my reputation, my position, my shop, and any chance to marry my beautiful Sarah. She was the apple of my eye, and I was hers'. She didn't care about my hand. Or did she? I couldn't bear her possible rejection, so when I was declared

tainted and driven out of town, I chose to leave without saying goodbye.

I became a wandering storyteller to earn money, and soon
my wit made a good enough living. Despite my hand, I mixed
with both wealthy and poor. In the heat of the day, I'd visit
souk and bazaar, pull up a stool and start a conversation with
the elders and city leaders.

One thing would invariably lead to another, and I'd wind
up starting a story. I'd pretend to tire about midway through
the telling, and my hosts would offer food, drink and maybe
a bed.

After a rest, I'd sit with the elders and merchants around
the fire and weave my tales. I had nothing and was almost
entirely content. Almost.

After a few years, I was paid handsomely to entertain
nobility. Apparently, my reputation preceded me in my travels.

My father always said, "How a man acts with those who
cannot help him tells a lot about a man's character." So, after
I'd been paid, I'd make it a point to help those less fortunate than myself. "Thank you for your kindness, storyteller," they'd say. I'd smile and quietly ask them to keep it to
ourselves. They always did, but when I did business in the
bazaar, I'd invariably find an extra measure of figs or wheat
or oil included with my purchase. What they didn't know was
I'd give that away too.

Others were worse off than me, and helping was the right thing to do. My father always said, too, "A candle is never harmed by lighting another candle."

But, you know, deep down I always hated my hand, so when I saw Jesus of Nazareth with his ragtag band of followers, I was intrigued. I'd heard he healed the sick and the blind, so I figured, at the very least, he could provide some inspiration for future stories. Someone said this Jesus was the Messiah, but, though all the scripture I'd contemplated indeed pointed to that possibility, I remained skeptical.

My excitement grew.

"Jesus, heal me," shouted a leper, but Jesus didn't hear him, so others took up the cry on his behalf. I watched Jesus declare the leper clean, and behold, he was.

Then suddenly Jesus was in front of me. "What is it that pains you so, storyteller? Tell me."

Despite my reservations, I found myself in tears, telling him of my cursed hand. I sobbed as I asked what I had done that had made God hate me.

He shook his head, smiled sadly, and said, "God loves you, friend. Stretch out your hand."

Instantly, my hand was healed. Can you fathom what it is like to see a miracle in front of you? A miracle performed on YOU?

As his group was walking off, Jesus healed a woman's sick daughter, then a beggar, paralyzed from the waist down since birth. He paused for a moment, then looked back, found me in the crowd, and beckoned me to join him.

One moment my hand was withered; the next I was made whole. Oy, who can resist following a miracle worker? Not me.

As time went by, I listened to Jesus and learned of God's love for everyone. And more importantly, I learned of God's grace and forgiveness towards me. I understood that Jesus was claiming to be God, and after everything I saw and experienced, I believed him. So did Sarah, when I bumped into her a few weeks later coming out of an olive oil merchant's stall. She had remained a maiden for me all these years, as I had been faithful to her.

Our reunion was glorious, and three days later I asked her to become my wife. Jesus was there when I proposed, and as his happy tears joined ours, his broad smile told us both that we were doing the right thing. Can you imagine the creator of the universe blessing our union?

I opened a carpentry shop in Jerusalem, and Jesus came in to help sometimes. After all, he had learned a few things from his father, also a carpenter. Now, between you and me, I was a much better woodworker, and he would joke that he would change my hand back to the way it was before if I outdid him again.

Sarah and I got busy with life, and although we were his disciples, we saw him less and less as he wandered through Galilee spreading his message. But we believed and told others, who in turn, believed too.

Then we learned that the Romans had arrested him and that the Jews asked for Barabbas to be freed, instead of Jesus. Pilate had ordered Jesus to be scourged and ultimately crucified.

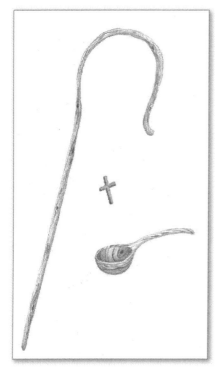

We fought the crowds and hurried to Golgotha. We watched him die, but his was not a death with hatred. It was a death with love.

For us.

During the earthquake, I heard the Centurion cry out in fear and wonder, "Surely this man was the Son of God." We spoke with him afterward, and later he became a believer also.

Sight restored. Lepers healed. Sicknesses cured. Paralytics walk. A little girl raised from the dead. Lazarus. The multitudes fed with just a few loaves and fishes. My withered hand made whole. Water turned into wine. We were saddened to the point of tears, but somehow we knew it was impossible for death to keep him.

And death couldn't hold Jesus.

He appeared to us a few days later, on Tuesday evening as Sarah and I were eating dinner. One moment he wasn't there, and the next he was. After our initial astonishment, we set another plate on the table. Jesus ate some bread, drank half a flagon of my most excellent beer, and enjoyed a hearty helping of rabbit lentil stew. He was alive again all right. He smiled, smacked his lips in his funny way and told Sarah her stew was seasoned to perfection. At the table, the three of us talked for a long while about life, heaven, and other things.

Then we moved to my workshop, where Sarah lit all our oil lamps, and we watched as Jesus finally bested my woodworking skill. I still have the shepherd's curved staff he made me. Jesus carved Sarah a beautiful wooden serving ladle too, and a tiny wooden cross she wears around her neck.

He blessed our child Sarah was carrying, although we had told no one yet, and she wasn't showing. A boy, he said, one destined for great things. He blessed our future children too. Then he prayed for us to remain steadfast in him, bid us shalom, and left. He didn't use a door.

We saw Jesus for the last time when he appeared to the multitude, and we watched him ascend into heaven.

Sarah and I waved to him as he ascended up into the clouds, and he waved back to us.

So now we are followers of The Way and bold proclaimers of the deity of Jesus. When folks from my old village come and try to argue with me about Jesus, I merely hold up my hand. That's pretty much all it takes to convince them. They ask, "What can we do to have eternal life?" I tell them to believe in their hearts that Jesus is Lord and confess with their mouth that God has raised him from the dead. Most do. I say Jesus will come again, not as a servant but as a king. I like that, and so do they.

✤ ✤ ✤

It's time to finish this story. Sarah has called our four children and me to dinner, and she is serving our family's favorite meal: bread, beer, and rabbit lentil stew.

Oh, and in case you were wondering, all our children have healthy hands.

Shalom.

Pure religion is love in action.

Centurion

I am the senior Centurion, commander of an entire army of Roman legionarii, the fiercest, ablest soldiers in the world. I am also the trusted counselor and confidant to Pontius Pilate, the Roman Governor of Judea. I was there when Pilate ordered Jesus's arrest, and there, too, when he spoke with the traveling preacher.

In my official capacity, I oversaw Jesus's scourging, although I would have gone anyway, for I was curious about him.

✤ ✤ ✤

Scourging is a vicious punishment that Rome metes out to deviants and lawbreakers. The number of lashes the prisoner receives is proportional to the seriousness of the offense. Meant to deter crime, it sometimes results in the prisoner's death from blood loss and shock. Society almost always gains.

But somehow this man, Jesus of Nazareth, was different. To me, he didn't seem to deserve such punishment.

During our afternoon meals together, Pilate and I sometimes talked about Jesus and how he and his growing band of followers were traveling about Galilee. My spies reported that he healed the sick, cured blindness, cast out demons and performed miracles. Two of my most trusted infiltrators reported the unbelievable claim that Jesus fed five thousand men with a few baskets of fishes and bread. They said Jesus was a gentle teacher, with a radically different way of thinking.

But imperial Rome wasn't interested in new philosophy, just in maintaining its ruling authority. After all, Jesus wasn't threatening Rome.

Then, members of the Jewish ruling council, the Sanhedrin, came to Pilate, saying that Jesus claimed to be the Son of God, and should be put to death for blasphemy. However, my informants said Jesus's teachings of love and forgiveness endangered the Sanhedrin's positions of power and wealth—and advised that this was but a religious issue. We again ignored such talk, for Rome allows for all kinds of gods. What difference is one more?

Pilate's opinion was that Jesus, despite his radical thinking and good works, was either a liar or mad. I mostly concurred, but one evening, in an introspective moment, I asked, "What if this man really is the Son of God?"

For a moment, Pilate stared at me. Cold fear flickered in his eyes. But then he laughed. "Come now, dear Centurion, you've had too much wine."

Perhaps I had.

Then the leaders of the Jews came to us saying Jesus had claimed to be the king of the Jews and would lead a rebellion against Rome.

This attracted our attention.

Rome cares not for religious spats in backwater regions like Judea, but one cannot call himself king without repercussions.

As Rome was the occupying force in Judea, the Jews were not allowed to have weapons, a standing army, or to execute prisoners. So, by default, punishments such as arrest, scourging, imprisonment, and crucifixion became our responsibility. And we were good at it.

Orders were given to apprehend and flog Jesus. I was there with ten of my soldiers late at night when he was captured in the garden. I didn't anticipate a fight, and there was none. Well, not much of one.

When that rodent of a man, Judas Iscariot, betrayed Jesus with a kiss of friendship and my men moved in to take Jesus into custody, one of Jesus's followers angrily struck out with a sword and cut off a servant's ear. To my amazement, Jesus sternly said, "No more of this." He picked up the ear, brushed off some particles of dirt, then put it back on the man's head. Healed.

Jesus was led away to our jail's central holding area, where my men beat him unmercifully. One of the Sanhedrin mockingly suggested we create a crown for him, the 'King of the Jews.' So, as a cruel joke, my soldiers wove a crown of fresh bramble thorns for the prisoner. The milky sap of the vine, mixed with sweat and blood, ran down his face and burned his eyes. Spines—some as long as my little finger—protruded from his scalp.

Then the real punishment began. How a man could endure such a scourging and live, I know not. His skin was hideously flayed by the cruel metal and stone barbs of the whip and lash. I could see bone in many places. My men showed no mercy, for they earned extra denarii for each scourging. Some enjoyed the task.

I wanted to turn away, but I did not, for I am the Centurion.

The pain and agony must have been unbearable, but Jesus held no malice towards his tormentors. This intrigued me, for I had witnessed many men, and a fair number of women, fall under the Roman lash. Invariably, the prisoner would curse their tormentors or beg for mercy. Or both.

Jesus did neither. Furthermore, I heard him tell my men that he forgave them, and in doing so, he earned my respect.

Later, I was there when Pilate interviewed Jesus the second time. My men had done their job well, for he was covered with gore and could barely stand. Pilate's wife counseled him to release Jesus, but instead, he gave the Jewish Sadducees and their mob what they wanted and condemned Jesus to death by crucifixion.

While Pilate was ceremonially washing his hands to signify removal of his guilt in this matter, Jesus looked at me for a long moment, and asked softly, "Who do you say I am, Centurion?"

I had to honestly confess, "I am not sure, Jesus of Nazareth."

To this, he replied, "You know of me. Listen and watch with your heart."

Shortly after, Jesus carried his cross up to Golgotha, the hill outside Jerusalem where crucifixions took place. My men placed his feet one on top of the other and drove long, iron spikes through them deep into the wood. They stretched his arms wide and drove nails through the palms of his hands to the cross beam. Because they had experience with crucifixions, they also roped his wrists to the wood lest the nails tear-free with his body weight. Then he was raised up for the public to see.

Pilate had commanded that a sign, 'King of the Jews,' be placed above Jesus's head. The Jews protested—but Pilate would not yield.

Naked, whipped almost till dead, and flanked by two other criminals on their crosses, Jesus lasted a mere six hours. His mother, a few of his followers, and a large number of townspeople had come to witness his death. I could hear them talking amongst themselves, speaking of the miracles Jesus performed throughout Judea. Sight restored. Lameness cured. Demons cast out. Sicknesses healed. One man, Lazarus, said he had been raised from the dead by Jesus.

There were dozens of witnesses to Lazarus's death—and return to life.

When Jesus passed, he cried out with a loud voice, "It is finished."

At that very moment, there was a tremendous earthquake. I was facing towards the city; to my astonishment, I saw the thick veil of the Jewish temple torn in two, from top to bottom. I lost my balance and, overwhelmed, fell to my knees. It all made sense to me now. I cried out, in some fear but mostly wonder, "Surely this man is the Son of God."

As the rumble of the earthquake was easing, a carpenter, Achim, and his wife, Sarah, helped me to my feet. As I thanked them, Achim said he had been born with a withered hand, and claimed Jesus had healed it. A small crowd gathered around us, and he held up his hand for all to see. Several people had known him since childhood and corroborated his story.

I examined it. Whole.

 I returned to my garrison, and though I had to deal with Pilate, I took time to consider all I had seen and heard. I posted guards around the tomb to allay the Jews claims that the body would be stolen by his followers. Then, on the third day, Jesus vanished from his grave, and my guards deserted their post. That never, ever happened, for the penalty for desertion was death.

I questioned the women who went to tend to his body early Sunday morning. They insisted that an angel had said he had risen, and that they had seen Jesus alive. My spies reported that Jesus appeared to his followers a few days after he supposedly came back to life. News of this incident spread like wildfire, and a movement called 'The Way' sprang up, so—called because Jesus once said, "I am the way, the truth, and the life. No man comes to the Father except through me." Dedicated to living by Jesus's teachings, it quickly spread throughout the region. In the months and years afterward,

I was amazed that even when gruesomely tortured nearly to death, ordinary people wouldn't recant their testimony that Jesus was alive.

Then two of my most capable junior officers approached me and said they wanted to leave the Legion and join The Way. I allowed this, and a few months later, privately made my own decision.

I, too, would become a follower of Jesus.

That is how I came to believe in the deity of Jesus of Nazareth. I have witnessed things I cannot explain, nor understand, which brought me to the inescapable conclusion that Jesus is God, and king of us all.

I called for an inspection of my troops for one last time. I felt I owed my soldiers an explanation of what was to come. These men would follow me to their certain death; they loved me, and I loved them. As they crowded around, I explained what I had seen, heard, and experienced. And my conclusion. Many confessed similar thoughts and publicly announced their allegiance to Jesus.

But Rome doesn't allow challenges to its authority.

And now, during the last few moments of my life, I, Centurion, kneel with both hands bound behind my back, my bruised head on a blood-slicked block of wood. And again, I proclaim that Jesus is the Son of God.

The End

Sometimes the best gain is to lose.

A Seat on the Council

My name is Saul of Tarsus, and of all the Jewish Pharisee religious zealots in the civilized world, I showed the most promise. I was hardly surprised, when, in my twenty-fourth year, I was called to an official meeting in the Council Room of the Sanhedrin. The room was huge, and almost all seventy-two members of the council were in attendance. "We have a special task for you, Saul," they said. "Do it well, and your admission to the ruling council of the Jews, the Sanhedrin, will be assured. You will be one of us." A hush fell over the room as the oldest and most famous member of the group, Hillel the Elder, leaned forward and cleared his throat. I was taken aback by the hatred etched on his weathered face. He pointed a gnarled finger at me. "Saul. We will give you what you need. Kill them. Persecute them. Imprison them. All of them. Do it within the law, do it righteously, but get rid of those Jesus followers."

"Get rid of them all."

I was born a Roman citizen and privileged son of a prominent Jewish Pharisee. My family moved to Jerusalem when I was thirteen, where I learned at the foot of revered Rabbi Gamaliel in the Hillel School in Jerusalem. Only the best and brightest gained admission—and of course I was the best and brightest of them all. The Torah and Talmud were child's play. I could recite and argue any Jewish position in Greek, Aramaic, and Hebrew. My mastery of any subject was boundless; my teachers seldom challenged me. My dedication and fervor for Jewish law were unparalleled, so it was natural that I became an attorney.

When I reached my twenty-third year, I married my wife, also from a prominent family. Sadly, when we had been husband and wife but six weeks, she fell to the cobbles from a third-story balcony when the railing she was leaning on collapsed. I rushed to her side, but she never awoke from her injuries. Ours was happiness so complete that when she passed, I was so overcome with grief that I resolved never to wed again.

My parents felt I needed a diversion from my anguish, so they urged me to accept the job I was offered. Being admitted to the Sanhedrin would be a reward for our strict observance of Jewish law and tradition. My esteemed family was already wealthy and belonged to society's elite; a position on the Sanhedrin would serve to enhance my family's prestige and fortune for generations to come.

I accepted the assignment.

From a rooftop garden with a view of Golgotha, I watched Jesus of Nazareth writhe on the cross. There was an earthquake, and I narrowly missed being crushed by a falling statue, but a slave girl next to me wasn't so fortunate. I held her head to comfort her as she passed. During her last moments, she looked deeply into my eyes, and said, not unkindly, "You are Saul, and you will soon know the truth." My heart skipped a beat, and I had a fleeting feeling of dread. Then she smiled through the pain and looked far past me. As she died, she whispered, 'Jesus.' I spat and cursed the name Jesus of Nazareth. Ordinary townspeople were in awe of this traveling preacher. Not me. The more I learned about Jesus, the more I hated him.

I saw how dangerous this Jesus was becoming to the stability of Jewish culture and our religious way of life; Jews were abandoning their religion to follow the Jesus movement, what they called 'The Way.' The Sanhedrin stressed that we must prevent this at any cost, for lessened temple taxes and reduced attendance at synagogue meant that our influence would also diminish And so I went about my task with a righteous fervor that surprised even me.

My ferocity and brutality were legendary, and I received enthusiastic support from the Council. Sometimes I had Jesus followers imprisoned, those who seemed like they might waver and recant their allegiance to the carpenter's son. We treated them however we wished, but mostly I condemned them to die for their heretical beliefs.

I gave my approval to the stoning of Stephen—after I had listened to his sincere but deluded appeal that Jesus was the Son of God. Stephen was willing to die for his belief; though I wouldn't admit it, I was impressed—and—unsettled. For the barest of moments, I thought that maybe there was something to his claim.

Angry with myself, I tried to put that feeling aside and worked even harder to satisfy the Council. My fury grew, like a voracious monster, demanding that I act ever more ruthlessly in persecuting followers of 'The Way.' In essence, I became a terrorist. A religious terrorist. And I asked for permission to travel to Damascus, where The Way was flourishing.

But then I had my own Jesus moment.

We left Jerusalem for Damascus in the wee hours of the morning. Traveling with my entourage, by early evening we were road weary and ready for an evening meal and some rest.

The second day was the same as the first.

On the third day, during the hottest part of the afternoon, we were making our way at the speed of donkeys when there was a flash of pure white light. I was knocked to the ground. I awoke in an enormous, white room. No, that's not entirely correct. I came to my senses in a blinding white world. Everything was white. Somehow, I knew I was in the presence of the Almighty. My eyes were burning, but I was not in pain. I heard a voice, powerful and true. It said to me, "Saul, Saul, why do you persecute me? Why do you kick against the goads?"

Goads. Was the Almighty saying I kick against the goads? I considered the analogy. When bulls are pulling the plow, sometimes they get ornery and kick back at the farmer. Over the years, farmers had installed a pointy, spear-like apparatus called goads behind the bull's hind legs. When the brute tried to kick its master, it received a painful reminder that there are consequences for bad behavior. Some animals never learned and lived a life of painful futility.

He was comparing me to the latter. Painful futility. That hurt.

I'm not one to argue with the Almighty, but I wanted to be sure. "Who are you, Lord." I said, using the term 'Lord' to acknowledge my inferior status.

"I am Jesus, whom you persecute."

Jesus of Nazareth was speaking to me, even though I saw Him die on the cross three years ago. I was confused. Is Jesus alive? How can that be?

Then, scenes of the past flashed through my mind. I saw the creation of the universe, the earth's formation, Adam and Eve in the garden, the flood, Moses leading the Israelites,

Solomon's opulence, and other events of the past. I saw prophets throughout the ages. Time sped up and slowed down—at the same time. I saw everything through the eyes of the Creator and felt his enormous love for humanity.

At that moment my life changed. I realized that Jesus, crucified, buried, and now risen from the grave, really is the Son of God.

His voice boomed again. "Now get up, and go into the city, where you will be told what to do."

I obeyed.

My life had changed in an instant. I went from persecuting Jesus followers to spreading the good news that Jesus is alive. I joined The Way and soon became one of its leaders. I endured beatings, floggings, hunger, imprisonment and other minor inconveniences for the sake of spreading the truth about Jesus. It's that important. Jesus is alive, and everyone, even Gentiles, can have what he offered.

Jesus even changed my name.

So, go forth like me, Paul of Tarsus, and shine like stars in the universe. For to live is Christ, and to die is gain.

The End

Be what you wish others to become.

First Responders

Seth walked up the hill, singing softly, his mellow baritone voice going ahead of him. "All clear tonight, my little four-legged friends. My little woolly friends, you are sleeping like babies. Good night my little woolly friends. Tomorrow is another day. Good night, to you, good night, to you..."

He walked over to our small fire and grunted as he sat in one of our three-legged folding chairs. He laid his staff on the ground next to him but kept his rod on his belt, at the ready. Hey, you never know. We weren't exactly in the wilderness, but we did have a bear carry off one of our ewes two weeks ago.

I tossed him a cup and the ladle. "Stew's good tonight, friend, and the wineskin is hanging from that tree right over there."

"Thanks. The fire feels great." He warmed his hands then looked up. "Tonight's going to be a bit colder than last." The August night sky was bracingly clear. We could see thousands of points of light and almost imagine a few constellations.

Suddenly Seth pointed overhead. "Look, there goes another streak—a greenish yellow one. And there goes a gold one. How beautiful. We're so lucky, Hiram. Here we are, outside on this beautiful night, watching over those trusting animals. I can almost feel the Lord's presence. He's guiding us along quiet waters. He's restoring our souls. We're shepherds, like the Lord. I like that."

Our flock lay quietly on a hillside just outside of Bethlehem. Somehow, we both felt we could relax tonight. Most of our sheep were asleep; a few baaed here and there. Little short bleats, the kind that says to the rest of the flock, "I'm here."

I tossed a few twigs on our little fire, more content than I had been all season. "I like that too. The part about the waters and our souls." I pulled my cloak around me and lay back against a gently sloping rock face, already drifting off. "Wake me in a few hours. And don't bother me about the sky. I see it every night, and nothing ever changes. Even your streaks of light." We laughed, and I wrapped my cloak around my head and closed my eyes.

In moments, I was asleep, albeit lightly. No shepherd worth his salt ever slept heavily while his flock was in the field.

Then we had our Jesus moment.

"Hiram." Seth's voice, strained and somewhat shrill, cut through my slumber and I stirred. It seems that I was only asleep for a few moments, and now the sun was up. I stretched, yawned and removed the cloak from my face.

"Sorry for overslee...," My sentence was cut short. Right in front of me was an angel, standing a few feet above our little campfire—in the air. The glory of the Lord shone all around him, so brightly that it dazzled my eyes. I looked to the left and right. Darkness. I could see the sleeping town of Bethlehem sprawled out at the base of the hillside. It was still the dead of night, and I must have slept for only a few minutes.

A star in the heavens shone radiantly over the little town; a ray of pure white light seemed to illuminate a particular area.

We were terrified. Seth moved and stood a little behind me. Thanks, Seth. I felt him poke my back. "Hiram. Hiram. Say something, Hiram." Irritated, I glanced back at him. He was so afraid he looked like he would throw up.

I found my voice, but it was as shaky as my knees and hands. "We're just simple shepherds, friend. What do you want with us?"

The angel said, "Do not be afraid. I bring you good news of great joy that will be for all the people. Today in the town of David a Savior has been born to you; he is Christ the Lord. This will be a sign to you: You will find a baby wrapped in cloths and lying in a manger."

Then there was a sound like tearing fabric, only louder and crisper. Over the angel's head was a multitude of angels, more than I could ever count in all my days. They were singing praises to God like this: "Glory to God in the highest, and on earth peace to those on whom his favor rests." It was beautiful.

They stayed for what seemed to be half of the night, singing glory to God. For a while, Seth and I rejoiced and sang too. Our voices, puny and flat, were made perfect by theirs. Then they disappeared, and it was night again.

I took a gulp of wine from the wineskin. Seth had one too, then another. Then I did, and again. Our shakes were almost gone. I asked him, "What should we do now?"

A sheep baaed—but to me, it sounded like 'Gooooo.' Another baaed, then another. In moments, the entire flock was baaing. But they all sounded like they were saying 'go.' In all my years of shepherding, I've seen sheep do stupid things, I've heard sheep make odd noises, but I've never heard a sheep, let alone an entire flock, say 'go.'

It had to be a sign.

Seth exclaimed, "They're all telling us to go. Let's go find the child, Hiram. Like the angel said."

We looked at our flock. With certainty, we knew they would be safe for the evening, so we gathered our cloaks, rods, and staffs, banked our fire and set off for Bethlehem.

It wasn't far. The star overhead illuminated our way, and we quickly found what we were seeking—the babe wrapped

in cloths, lying in a manger—just like the angel told us. His parents, Joseph and Mary, welcomed us with open arms. "He shall be named Jesus on the eighth day," they said. We told them about the angel, who said the child would be our Savior, Christ the Lord. Mary nodded, and Joseph explained all that had happened to bring them to this spot. We were amazed, and, eventually, as we made our way back to our flock, we told everyone we met on this beautiful night.

And in that way, we lowly shepherds met *the* Good Shepherd, who will lead us beside quiet waters and will restore our souls. We both liked that.

The End

Happy Birthday, baby Jesus.

Tempest

My boat, *Hegai*, is longer, wider, and stronger than most craft here on the Sea of Galilee. It has a deeper draft too, which makes it harder to navigate shallow waters, but better for rough seas. *Hegai* means 'The Force' in Hebrew, and everyone who has ridden in it agrees that the name perfectly suits the vessel. It has a small canvas cabin in the stern to escape the elements.

My grandfather built this vessel from cedar and oak, and it has been in the family ever since. Since I grew up on this boat, I know every mortise and tenon joined inch of it. I know exactly what it can do, for I have been sailing it for nigh thirty years. Sometimes I fish for my livelihood, but mostly I rent the vessel out to transport goods or groups of people across the lake.

Some fourteen miles long and about seven miles wide at its broadest, the 'Sea' of Galilee is really a large freshwater lake. It is relatively shallow, but the bottom slopes gradually to an impressive depth in the middle. Once, when I was a foolish lad, and the water was uncommonly clear, I held on to the anchor line as we threw it over in the center of the lake. Eyes open as I sank, I held my breath and watched the sunlight dim around me; my world turned a shade of greenish blue.

With a sudden jerk, the hundred-foot-long anchor line stopped well shy of the bottom. I had heard stories of sea monsters from my grandfather and other sailors, and, with my sharp gutting knife at hand, I was ready for them. But happily, the monsters left me alone, and I slowly rose to the surface to a hero's welcome.

The Jordan River flows into the Sea of Galilee from the north and flows out of it to the south. To walk around it with its meandering shorefront road would take maybe a day and a half or two. To cut across the lake in my boat takes just a few hours, so I charge a tidy sum for the convenience.

Flanked to the east and west are high hills, almost mountains, that have a dramatic effect on the usually placid waters of the sea. Sometimes, when conditions are right, cold, dry air swoops down from the heights to the east and mixes with the warm, humid air over the lake. When that happens, tremendous storms form in an instant and, if not recognized and dealt with, can be deadly. Quickly seeking safe harbor is a must, and woe to the crew caught on the sea during such an event.

Once, I encountered waves churned up to seven feet, and almost lost *Hegai* as a result. I was fortunate that day. Every five or six years we lose a boat and its crew, once again proving that the seafaring proverb, 'there are no old, bold sailors' is true indeed.

One day, a group of men approached me to ferry them across the sea to the ten cities of the Gerasenes in the Gentile Decapolis on the far side. It had been unbearably hot for a week, and I could see clouds that bring cold weather slowly forming to the east. I had some misgivings, for, in my judgment, conditions were ripe for nasty squalls to form.

Several of the men said they were fishermen by trade and commented favorably on my boat. Those same men also studied the sky and the waters, then looked questioningly at each other. I noticed their interactions and told them that if they were concerned, we could go in the morning. They asked my opinion about the weather. Reading the weather is a skill all sailors gain and refine with experience, so I studied the sky again and felt the chill winds coming down from the heights. I didn't like it and told them. Their leader stepped forward and insisted that they would be fine, that the most that would happen is that we would get a little wet from the rain. The others deferred their judgment to him and, after a brief dickering about the price of passage, we set sail.

At first, due to an overabundance of caution, I purposely stayed closer to the shore than I would under normal conditions. But then we were making good time, about two-thirds through our voyage, and despite some ominous clouds forming, I elected to seek deeper water and a more direct route. I thought we would beat the storm—by a few hours at least.

How wrong I was.

At first, the storm seemed manageable. Then the wind rose against us, and the experienced sailors aboard looked to me for permission to drop the sail. I gave the command, and it was done professionally, neatly, and they stowed it away with a minimum of effort. Clearly, these men knew what they were doing. Then, without urging or orders, they took up oars. We still made headway despite rising waves and wind.

Their leader, a carpenter by trade, had taken residence in the canvas shelter, where he was fast asleep. I admired the man's casual attitude, for we had about a third of our journey to go against worsening conditions.

Suddenly, the sky became as night as the tempest significantly increased in magnitude. Tremendous winds swooped down and roared past our boat. Waves, some almost taller than my head when I was standing amidships, tossed *Hegai* around like a cork. Incredulous, I noticed the top of the mast bend. Since talking, even shouting, was impossible, I pointed to it.

Tiny pellets of hail stung our faces and exposed skin. Lightning flashed close overhead, and the peals of thunder were deafening. I noticed, on the top of the mast and boom, pale yellow sparks and purple strings of lightning dancing about. I motioned for Andrew, the closest and strongest of the fishermen, to help me at the helm, for it had become impossible to steer the craft alone.

A wave crashed over our bow, and we started to take on water. In moments, the boat settled lower into the sea despite furious bailing by the passengers. Then, illuminated by the lightning flashing overhead, we could see a tremendous wave rushing towards us fast. While still far away, we could tell that it was higher than the top of the mast.

We were in trouble. Bad trouble. I thought we were going to drown.

Until I had my Jesus moment.

In terror, the men cried out to Jesus, who was sleeping on a cushion in the canvas shelter. Sleeping. He awoke, stood straight up, looked at the towering wave and rebuked the storm.

Immediately the wave disappeared, and the storm ceased.

The storm did not just slowly abate. Instead, at that very instant it *stopped*. One moment we were going to drown, the next there was no storm whatsoever. The sky cleared, the sun came out, and there was a tiny breeze from behind us.

A trio of decent sized fish, flopping on the bottom of the boat, was the only sound to be heard. Jesus looked about at his friends and asked, "Where is your faith?" Then he went back to sleep.

All of us, especially me, was amazed at what he had done and trembled in fear at his power. I spoke with my passengers, who revealed themselves to be disciples of Jesus. They said this man was the Son of God. They said he healed sicknesses, cast out demons and raised a child from the dead. One fisherman, Peter, said that after a fruitless night of fishing, Jesus told them to cast their nets on the other side of the boat. Peter said he knew there weren't any fish there, but they obeyed anyway. The catch, Peter noted, had strained the nets almost to the breaking point.

And here, now, Jesus had calmed the tempest. Never before had I seen a storm just *stop*.

We were blown far off course by the winds, so we unfurled the sail again and made our way slowly towards our destination. As everyone was exhausted from fighting the storm, one by one they drifted off to sleep. I was the only one awake. After a while, Jesus joined me at the helm.

We spoke for what seemed like hours, and I asked him every question I could think of about being the Son of God, heaven, angels, prophecy and the like. I liked his answers and asked if I could join him.

He smiled and said, "Sure."

Then, as we neared our destination, I asked Jesus if we were really in any danger from the storm. He laughed and said no, that he's tending to the Father's business and nothing, he said, nothing would keep him from going where he must go.

And nothing did.

The End

All I see teaches me to trust the Creator for all I do not see.

The Children's Bread

A gurgling sound from across our single-room home caused me to turn. Miryam, our seven-year-old daughter, was bent double and slowly falling forward. I caught her in my arms, and, cradling her thin little body, dropped to my knees. She wept softly, silently, and so did I. Then, rocking her in my lap, I quietly hummed our love song. She calmed, then slowly kept time with my words by tapping and caressing my wrist. I loved that, for it meant she was singing along in her own way. Miryam shook her fist at her head and pointed to her throat and mouth. I nodded, as hot tears again streamed down our cheeks. The thing that lived within her had prevented my sweet daughter from speaking.

Again.

It wasn't always this way. When she was just a baby, Miryam had the most delightful laughter I've ever heard. Our daughter was so full of joy and love that many remarked she was the perfect child.

And she was.

We were content with our lives in Canaan. Keret, my husband, owned a thriving business extracting purple pigment from shellfish, which was used to make dye to color royal garments; I tended our garden and sold eggs from our small chicken farm. We were surrounded by friends and looked forward to raising our daughter until my husband was selected to be a male priest at the temple. We worshiped the moon goddess in our home, so we were excited about this honor. One evening several months into his tenure, when Miryam was four, he came home from the temple, despondent to the point of tears. He announced that the priestess was to sacrifice Miryam to our deity come the full moon in the next lunar cycle. Horrified, I slapped Keret's face as hard as I could and would have again, but he caught my hand and stopped me. I threw myself on our straw mattress and almost threw up.

I cried and screamed that the goddess had never required human sacrifices before, but he said that for the harvest to be plentiful next year, the high priestess said human blood was needed this year. He joined me on the mattress and held me.

His agony was more than mine, for our child had been chosen to honor *him*.

I was beside myself. Sacrifice our only child so crops might grow next year? I became furious—and also very scared. Surely not, I screamed. What if we had another invasion of locusts? What if our crops developed the orange rust and withered away? What then? Miryam was our only child, but not because we elected to have only one. We had lost three other babies to stillborn birth: two sons and a daughter. I had been unable to conceive again though not for diligent lack of effort. Suddenly, Keret jumped off the mattress and said there might still be a way. Without even putting on his sandals he ran out of our house. He came back about two hours later with his left hand tightly wrapped in a bloody bandage. In a voice hoarse with pain, he said that he had convinced the high priestess to wait three years until Miryam was seven years of age. In the interim, we were to sacrifice a bullock and a ram to the goddess each year until then. Unfortunately, the high priestess said that Miryam had to be rendered mute by a temple imp tomorrow morning, to not spoil our daughter's three-year purification process with meaningless babble. They could not sacrifice a child who speaks. How stupid this whole sacrifice thing was, we thought, but we were powerless to stop it.

I asked him what happened to his hand. He said the high priestess required blood to ensure the harvest was successful. He offered two fingers of his left hand, and she accepted. I wept bitterly, but my heart filled with love for my man. He said he just bought us some time—but we still needed to take her to the temple tomorrow.

Desperately, we tried to think of a way out, but alas, in the mid-morn, Miryam was taken from us to the temple. Amidst a grand ceremony, they subjected her to the darkness inside. When we got her back, she rocked in the corner and cried silently for three days. We held her, we tried to coax sounds from her throat, but she was unable to speak or even utter a sound. Worse still, sometimes when we looked in her eyes, we could almost see an entity lurking there. The imp.

And it was a dark and evil one at that.

But the imp wasn't visible always, and we tried to ignore it. But ignoring it didn't make it go away.

Miryam could still hear, though. They hadn't thought to take her ears, and I was overjoyed. I prayed at the temple and offered more silver to change her mind, but alas my prayers were met with stony silence.

They did, however, keep my silver.

Our days turned to ashes as despair and pain entered our household. We decided to stop worshiping the goddess. Who in their right mind could worship such a deity? So we could not slip away into the night, the temple posted armed guards outside our home and accompanied Miryam whenever she went outside. Many of our friends abandoned us, but some stood beside us and became our strength. My husband crafted a language that Miryam could speak with her fingers. With pantomime and words spelled out by hand, we could even have a conversation of sorts.

Three years sped by, and as the fateful lunar date grew closer, we became increasingly despondent. I offered the goddess my fingers too; they rejected me. Miryam was to be taken from us and murdered. We made fantastic plans of robbing the temple treasury and running away to Egypt. Another laughable fantasy was that the goddess herself would appear to pardon our daughter.

Keret crafted two daggers from a plowshare for us to kill the priestess with then commit suicide the same night Miryam was sacrificed to the moon goddess. Evil works both ways.

Then we had our Jesus moment.

Three months before the ceremony, friends told us about a traveling Jewish preacher named Jesus. Rumor had it that he healed the sick, the lame, and the blind. Some swore he was the Messiah, the Son of God, and had the power to forgive sins, and cast out demons. That last part caught our attention. One of my neighbor's children had been born lame; the next time I saw her she was dancing around her parent's stall in the bazaar praising Jesus, and I was astounded. Another friend had an apple-sized tumor on his neck healed as if it were never there. Others reported similar healings, a lot of them, and I began to have hope for Miryam.

We liked what we'd heard about Jesus's message of love and forgiveness, and decided to see him as soon as we could. A week before the ceremony, Miryam started to have seizures. Twice we witnessed her floating above her bed. We found dried blood on a sharp piece of metal in her nightclothes and remembered our neighbor's report of a mutilated goat four days past. Sometimes she looked at us with an unholy gaze and refused to 'talk.'

We became fearful of our daughter.

Then there was a terrible accident at the well. A young boy had fallen in; when they fished him out, he was very pale, and his head was at an unnatural angle. We wept, for he was very near death. However, his parents, followers of the Jewish preacher, swiftly brought him to Jesus.

I was there when the child walked back home.

Then it was two days before they were to take our daughter's life.

Even though Jews seldom interacted with Canaanites like us, in desperation, I decided to throw tradition to the wind and seek this Jesus. I found him ambling along with his band of followers. I witnessed him healing the sick and blessing those without hope, and I became a believer. I knew Jesus could heal Miryam. I just knew it.

The crowd around him was multiplying so fast that in a few moments I would be pushed away and all chance to speak to him would be lost. I might be a Gentile woman and lower than a Jew, but my daughter's life was in the balance, and I refused to be ignored.

I cried out, "Lord, Son of David, have mercy on me. My daughter is demon-possessed." To my chagrin, Jesus and his disciples kept walking. But I kept calling out to him. My voice grew shrill with the effort. His disciples urged him to walk away, and the crowd had begun to grumble. I pushed my way through the crowd, enduring several well-placed elbows. Finally, I was before him and out of breath. "Lord, Son of David, have mercy on me. My daughter is demon-possessed."

Jesus looked at me and, not without compassion, replied, "I came for the lost sheep of Israel."

I knelt, and tears ran down my face. I couldn't believe what I was hearing. Jesus had just healed Gentiles, and now he was telling me he was only here for Jews?

"Lord, help me." My heart was in tatters.

But again, he put me off. "It is not right to take the children's bread and give it to dogs."

At my wit's end, I was crumbling. How could my Jesus deny me?

Still, I believed, and in my heart, I bowed before his throne. I could barely breathe, for I felt like Miryam's demon was choking *my* throat. Spots flashed before my eyes. Then I had an inspiration. I had been to many feasts. The dogs that lay under the tables were the smartest. And fattest.

I managed to squeak, "Yes Lord, but even the dogs eat the crumbs from the Master's table."

He looked at me and smiled, "Woman, your faith is great. Let it be done as you desire." At that very moment, I knew in my heart that he had removed the demon from Miryam, and I hugged his knees in worship. His disciples gently lifted me to my feet, and I thanked him with all my heart. He smiled again, wiped away my tears, then was lost in the crowd.

When I returned home, I found Miryam sitting quietly in her daddy's lap on the long bench. I took her from him into my lap and stroked her hair. I kissed her forehead, and she smiled up at me. Her eyes were bright, shiny, and clear. I knew something was different.

Her voice, pure and sweet, broke the silence. "Mama, I am healed. The bad thing is gone from me, and it'll never come back." I wanted to yell with happiness and run around the room, but I kept my head. "That's wonderful, my darling.

Jesus healed you, and, because you can speak, you will not be sacrificed to the moon goddess."

Keret wrapped his strong arms around us both. Miryam began to sing our love song, along with corresponding caresses and taps on my wrist. When I stopped sobbing, I joined in. After a moment so did my husband.

And we sang our love song for a very long time.

The End

If you must doubt, doubt your doubts—never your beliefs.

Stepfather

My father, Jacob, was a carpenter, so in the tradition of our people, I became a carpenter too. We crafted wagon wheels, doors, chairs, tables and much more in his shop. But he also taught me how to see the hidden beauty of the wood and expose its full magnificence. There was nothing in the whole world I enjoyed more than seeing the potential in a pile of rough-hewn planks or a gnarled, wind-blown tree trunk and transforming it into a thing of splendor. Once, when I was eleven, my father commented on my passion. "You love the wood, Joseph. Not many do. Always remember, if you treat it with gentleness, insistence, and, sometimes, firmness, the wood will love you right back."

Alaish, my father's worker, chimed in, "Your father's right, Joseph," he said, "But don't forget, too, that the wood surprises, and sometimes disappoints." He clapped me on my back and continued. "But sometimes, just sometimes, it will delight you beyond your wildest dreams. Just like a woman".

They both laughed at Alaish's comment, and so did I, but I was young.

We grew up in Nazareth, and I had known Mary all my life. I'd see her now and again, running errands or walking with her family. A year younger than me, we would smile, and we would gaze into each other's eyes.

I thought about her often, but as I worked hard in my father's carpentry shop, the years passed quickly. Then, in the month of my sixteenth birthday, my parents started pointing out women of marrying age. Although marriages were customarily arranged by the father of the groom, my parents quietly deviated from tradition and allowed me to choose my wife. "Make a wise choice, Joseph," they said. But my sisters, on the other hand, would point out the girls becoming women, and comment. 'Malia? That one seems nice but she's nasty, and the one beside her, Bela, is lazy'. Teasingly, they pointed out another, Dabria, a dull, short, stout girl with wide hips and a crooked countenance. "Good for childbearing, Joseph," they'd say and laugh at my discomfort.

But Mary was always the one I desired. She was tall and slim. Her soft, silky ringlets of copper burnished mahogany hair sometimes escaped her headscarf and curled down towards her jaw. I liked the way her locks nuzzled the gentle curve of her neck.

When I spoke with her—which was as often as I could without seeming to be too insistent, my heart sometimes skipped a beat, and I hoped that she harbored the same feelings. My parents approved of her, my sisters just giggled, and one day I made my move.

Although I was secretly terrified, I went to her father and asked for her hand in marriage. He hugged me and accepted, saying that they had discussed my name in his home for some time and that they had discretely turned down two other suitors. I gave them the customary bridal payment, and at that moment Mary and I became betrothed. To my surprise, Mary's mother kissed my cheek and welcomed me to their family. My heart leaped at the family's reception, and when Mary came in, she smiled sweetly, blushed and turned away. But when she looked back at me with her thoughtful, soft brown eyes, I knew we would be happy together.

About six months later, Mary's elderly aunt Elizabeth became pregnant. At the same time her husband, Zechariah, was struck mute by an angel during his temple ceremony. Mary went to visit them at their home in the hill country of Judea.

A week after her departure, her father told me that Mary was with child.

She was supposed to be a virgin, and we had not consummated our marriage.

I was torn asunder.

I ran away and immersed myself in work and prayer in the workshop. My father and Alaish had the kind courtesy of staying away so I could deal with my pain, but they would leave food for me on the table just inside the front door.

I started—and left unfinished—doors, tables, and other carpentry projects. The wood I loved so much had become stingy and uncooperative. My beloved's face stared back at me from the grain. Graceful swirls in the bark reminded me of her hair. Life would never be the same.

In the evening of the second day, I decided to divorce Mary and move on in life. Undoubtedly there was another woman for me. When I went to bed that night, I gathered my cloak tightly around me and drifted off to sleep as the fire in the hearth burned down to dark red embers.

Then, early the next morning, I had my Jesus moment.

As I slept, an angel stood before me in a dream. He told me that Mary was with child from the Holy Spirit, not from a man. He said, "Joseph son of David, do not be afraid to take Mary home as your wife because what is conceived in her is from the Holy Spirit. She will give birth to a son, and you are to give him the name Jesus because he will save his people from their sins."

I was dumbfounded, and a bit hurt. I cried, "Why Mary, why me, why now?" He explained that I was the one because I am righteous in God's eyes and that my lineage is the house of David. He gently led me through the scriptures, and I accepted all he had to say.

Mary and I were to raise the child as our own. I was to be the stepfather to the savior of mankind.

I was stunned, humbled, and honored. And, I was relieved that Mary had not betrayed me, for God had chosen us to do his work. As my dream was ending, I asked the angel what I should do. He smiled and shrugged. "Do what you've always done, Joseph. Honor and obey God."

I awoke to the sound of doves cooing outside my workshop and found my breakfast sitting on the table. Fig cakes sprinkled with honey, wheat bread still warm from the hearth, and pickled quail eggs that had never tasted so good. The fire had been recently tended and crackled merrily. I said silent thanks to my father.

After prayers, I made my way home and told my parents of my dream. At first, they thought I was kidding, but then they agreed that I must honor God. They warned me that the village would speak harshly of Mary and me. I asked them to keep our conversation to ourselves, and they agreed.

Mary's pregnancy was becoming visible when she returned from her visit to her cousin Elizabeth. When I learned of her arrival, I asked her to walk with me. At first, neither of us spoke, but then we stopped at a large rock, and I told her of my dream. After, I quietly tried to tell her my feelings, but she put a finger to my lips and spoke of *her* angelic visit. I held her close and breathed in the smell of her hair. She gently stroked the back of my neck and murmured, "You are my husband, Joseph. I could never be untrue."

I replied, "And you are my wife, Mary. Always."

We were one once again.

We looked at each other, almost unable to believe our situation. I said, "We must honor and obey God, for this is what the angel said." With tears in her eyes, she replied, "We shall."

Her pregnancy quickly became *the* hot topic in Nazareth. My friends pleaded with me to divorce her. To their amazement, I stubbornly defended Mary, once to the point of knocking a good friend to the ground after he insisted she should be stoned her for adultery. He accepted my apology after I picked him up, and I refused to discuss the matter with anyone, even the rabbi. It was my decision, and mine alone, I said. Mary's and my family grew very close as we fended off well-meaning advice and not so thinly veiled insults.

Meanwhile, Mary's baby belly grew.

About that same time, King Herod of the Jews, obeying the Roman Emperor Augustus, ordered a census of the world. The head of each family was to make their way to their ancestral home and register. We lived in Nazareth but our family's origin was in Bethlehem, so I had to travel there to comply. The distance was roughly ninety miles, over rough terrain. I expected to push hard and complete my journey in record time, for Mary was to deliver within the next few weeks. The evening before I left, she came to me and informed me that she would go along, riding side saddle on our donkey. As I started to protest, I saw her soft brown eyes harden and turn a shade darker. "I will go with you, my husband. We will not be apart again." We hugged, and my heart melted. Morning found us on the road to Bethlehem.

We joined a group of travelers headed the same way, for there was safety in numbers against robbers. After a week, Mary started having pains and needed to stop and rest more often. The baby was making his presence known, she'd say. Our fellow travelers reluctantly bade us farewell and pressed on, for they couldn't wait for us each time. Finally, in the late afternoon of the tenth day, when we could see Bethlehem in the distance, Mary announced that the baby was coming soon. My exhaustion gave way to fear and panic, and I picked up our pace almost to a run until Mary made me stop. She said, "Joseph, Joseph, dear husband, we still have a little time." I felt better, but I still went much faster than before. We made it into town as evening fell. My anxiety grew again as I went to all the inns and quite a few private homes—but each turned me away. Every room had been taken by travelers like us who had come to register for the census. I banged on the same doors again and pleaded with the innkeepers. Finally, one took pity on us and offered his stable in a shallow cave. I gratefully accepted. About two hours after we got unpacked and settled, Mary delivered the baby by herself. I helped as best as I could, but my experience was with wood, not infants.

Around midnight two shepherds came to us in the stable. Mary had placed the child in a manger so he might sleep, and the shepherds gazed upon him with awe and reverence. An angel had told them about the birth, they said, and they had come to worship the King of Kings. When I asked how they had found us, they said that an angel told them to look for a babe, wrapped in cloths, lying in a manger. And, a star, brighter than all the others in the heavens, had lit the way with its pure, white light. I looked up; to my amazement, there was a star overhead that seemed to be shining directly on our stable.

When the shepherds departed, our little family lay back in the straw, warmed by the body heat of the animals whose home we shared. Mary, holding Jesus, fell asleep instantly. For a long while, I contemplated them both, with wonder.

As I drifted off to sleep, I promised God that I would be the best father that I could be. At that same time, Jesus made a soft sound as he slept. I took it as a confirmation from my stepson, the Son of God.

The End

It is not the greatness of my faith that moves mountains,
but my faith in the greatness of God.

The Best for Last

When I was a boy, my best friend lived two doors down. His name was Jesus.

✤ ✤ ✤

When Joseph and Mary brought their family from Egypt to Nazareth, my village was reluctant to accept them. My parents told me that Mary had conceived Jesus out of wedlock, but Joseph cherished her as his wife regardless of what the community said or thought. I didn't know what 'out of wedlock' meant, but Grandfather Levi said that it was a bad thing, and to overlook it took a special man. Grandfather also said that he could look into a man's eyes and see his heart. He always maintained Jesus's daddy, Joseph, was the most excellent man he had ever met.

My grandparents embraced Joseph and Mary like their own. As time went by, my parents and the rest of the village did too.

We were the eldest sons of our families, Jesus, and I. We were also roughly the same age. Being boys, we sought each other's company, because girls were still mysterious and we were ill at ease around them. To us kids in the neighborhood, Jesus was just another boy—awkward sometimes, sometimes great at throwing rocks and playing games.

His deity was hidden during our childhood, except maybe for the time several of us boys found a sparrow laying in his courtyard. I wanted to pluck its flight feathers and put them in my sister's hair, but he said no, the bird was just sleeping. When he picked it up, it stirred, chirped once and flew away. We looked at him, uncomprehending. He shrugged, and we forgot about the incident till much later in life.

Growing up, Jesus spent a great deal of time in his father's woodworking shop, where he learned the trade. Now, Jesus was good with wood, really good, but a cousin from another town told us of a boy with a withered hand, who, at our age, was well on his way to becoming a brilliant craftsman. We kidded Jesus mercilessly that he had competition until he chased us down, tackled us and rubbed our faces in a rotten pumpkin. Later that day I found a seed in my ear.

My friends and I laughed about that, and still do.

As we grew up, Jesus began to spend time teaching in the synagogue, and our paths crossed less and less. I attended a few of his lectures, and his knowledge of the Torah was astonishing. I was proud of my friend, and a little confused. How did he know so much?

Since I was the eldest son in my family, I decided to follow my father's footsteps into the family's winemaking business. By age twenty-five, I'd learned all there was to know about making wine in Judea. Then, with my uncle Samuel and his son Isaac, we started traveling all over the world, sampling grapes, discussing growing methods, meeting fellow winery owners and introducing myself as heir to my father's business. I had a lot to learn, and I applied myself to the task.

But every time I returned home and looked up my old friends, Jesus was always the first one I'd seek.

My family's business supplied wines of all kinds to everyone according to their price range. Our best seller, a low alcohol jug wine, was thin and sweet and was meant for everyday consumption. We shipped these in twenty, thirty, or sixty-gallon earthenware jars. Better wines were stored in smaller amounts in Roman amphorae; a particular type of container lined both inside and outside in pitch and plaster.

My favorite wine to make, and drink, was fermented in an exclusive stone vat and stored for a few years in a 'V' shaped container. During each stage of the process, I'd introduce cardamom, juniper berries, and honey taken from beehives in the nearby pink lavender fields. After a while, it's intense ruby-garnet color would set this wine apart from the other wines in our lineup. The last stage was the most important of all. That's when I added my secret ingredients that make my wine both sweet and salty, smooth and biting, silky to the nose and pleasant to the tongue at the finish. I was very proud of my product, and I drew small amounts when it was ready. Jesus loved my wine, and he crafted a beautifully ornate cedar chest for me to store it in. In turn, I shared it liberally, with him and his family.

In early winter, a very wealthy man in Canna contracted with us to provide wine for his son's wedding feast in the upcoming fall, after the harvest. This celebration was to be a grand affair, spanning seven days of festivities. They had invited many dozens of guests, and all were sure to be thirsty. Spare no expense, he said. Even when we presented him with an estimation of charges, he merely glanced at it, snapped his fingers and approved it without hesitation. Then, after sampling my personal wine, to my amazement, he smiled and instructed us to add another twenty percent profit, for he had great faith in both our wines and servants.

The earnings from this seven-day job would be enough to buy a neighboring vineyard, its associated presses, and to construct several new storage cellars for its yield.

We got right to work.

Our field workers and those involved in the production process labored day and night. Through the careful mixing of grapes and batch, we increased both the quality and quantity of our wines. We developed a new technique to ensure one batch be the same quality as the next, something extraordinarily difficult to do when producing large quantities of wine.

Finally, we had more than enough. The day was almost upon us, and we were ready.

We bought an old storage building just a few miles from the feast site, and another, a half day's journey away, explicitly to store the feast wines. The closer building was in dire need of repair, and we had to shore up one of its walls. After the feast, we were going to tear it down and build another. All it had to do was last for a little while.

It didn't.

Disaster struck around noon on the second day of the wedding feast. My servants and I were at the old building, busily sorting new wine for the celebration and dealing with the empty containers. Then, one of our donkeys was threatened by a viper that had slithered out from a crack in the shored-up wall. The snake struck, missed, and coiled again. The donkey, harnessed to an empty cart, went berserk. Braying madly, it reared up on its hind legs and crushed the snake with its front hooves. Then the panicked animal raced wildly around the inside of the building.

Still tethered to the terrified animal, the cart tipped over and smashed everything it touched, including three of the four supports for the weak wall. With a creaking groan, it fell with a heavy thump into the center of the building. Next, the roof collapsed, followed by the remaining walls. We had stacked most of the wine away from the weak wall, right next to the last wall that collapsed. We could salvage nothing.

I did a quick headcount of workers inside. Fortunately, no one was injured. Even the donkey had escaped. But in a few seconds, a year of effort and many months of planning were ruined.

Walking around the dusty rubble, stunned, I could only think of one thing: the wedding feast would run out of wine within the hour.

I sent a servant on my fastest horse to notify my father of what had happened, and to speed delivery of wine from the far warehouse to the feast for tomorrow. If they managed to get the wine there in time, the next day could be salvaged. I told my servant, too, to see if we had enough wine stored in our personal wine cellar to cover this afternoon, although I doubted it. I mounted a horse and, with a heavy heart, set off for the wedding feast. I dreaded what was to come next.

Then I had my Jesus moment.

I arrived through the back gate and went directly into the storage area to check our stock on hand. Depleted. Then I went to be the outdoor courtyard, where most of the guests were mingling. Jesus caught my eye and beckoned me to join him, his mother, and his disciples. But I waved him off. Later.

I found the bridegroom sitting one table adjacent to where Jesus was reclining, and, upon hearing my bad news, the man became visibly upset. I was supposed to have delivered a shipment of wine, and I had shown up empty-handed. Mary, Jesus's mother, overheard my conversation with the groom and informed Jesus that the wine had run out. Jesus looked directly at me, sighed, then turned to her and said that his time had not yet come.

Mary ignored him and told the servants to do whatever Jesus said.

Over to the side were several large stone jars, used for ceremonial washing. Jesus quietly told the servants to fill them with water. Then he asked someone to take a ladle of it to the master of the ceremony, who had just come into the room and was unaware of my predicament. As the master sipped the liquid, his eyes widened, and he grinned. He remarked to the bridegroom that he had never tasted such good wine before—and was surprised that the groom had saved the best wine for last.

In a matter of just a few moments, Jesus had turned water into wine. The wedding celebration was saved, and so were we.

Now, remember, I know my trade. It takes months of growing, harvesting, processing, and fermentation to produce a drinkable beverage. For some odd reason, I remembered the sparrow in that backyard so long ago—the one Jesus had taken in his hand. I looked at him with wonder and said thank you. He smiled, then reached up and pretended to pull a pumpkin seed out of my ear. We laughed for a long time.

Later I examined the stone jars and sampled Jesus's wine. To my utter surprise, I found it to be *far* superior to my best efforts, unquestionably the most excellent wine I'd ever tasted. The stone jars were large enough to supply the evening's wine, and the next day my father came through with more wine from our far warehouse.

I was there when Jesus performed his first miracle, and I also witnessed countless others after I left my family's business and became a follower of The Way.

Now I'm an old man, and I often think of that day in Cana. Though I searched, I've never found a wine like Jesus made that miraculous afternoon. Some things just cannot be improved upon, especially when the Son of God, my childhood best friend from two doors down, creates it.

The End

Measure your life by loss instead of gain; not
by the wine drunk but in the wine poured forth,
for love's strength stands in love's sacrifice;
and who suffers most has most to give.

Stone Thrower

When a nation conquers another nation, the winners usually kills the loser's soldiers and enslaves the civilian population. That's just the way it works. That's how I became a slave.

My name is Caleb, and I was a gold merchant's eldest son. My siblings and I enjoyed a good life and received our education in the best schools with children from many cultures. While philosophy bored me, and I was only fair in mathematics, I found my talent in languages.

Almost all of my childhood friends were boys and girls from other lands; we enjoyed many meals with them in each other's homes. Happy confusion sometimes reigned at dinner time as our parents pretended they didn't know where we were or who was coming to our house to share our meals. All we children knew was that there was great respect for each other and harmony between families. Each set of parents made it fun for visiting children to learn to read and write their language. By age thirteen, in addition to my native tongue, Greek, I was fluent in Latin and Aramaic.

Then another country coveted our nation's rich gold mines and invaded our land.

My people were great miners but lousy warriors. My father, conscripted into the army early on, was killed in the third attack. We went on to lose every battle and eventually the war. Our people became human livestock in the slavery trade, bought and sold in the souks and bazaars of the world. My mother and sisters, fair and pleasing to the eye, were peddled to a wealthy sheep merchant. I watched Matthias, my little brother, march up a plank to a slave ship set to sail west in two days. With tears running down our faces, we waved farewell, and he received a fast clout to the side of his head for saying goodbye.

Rumor had it that my group of slaves were to go on overland in two weeks to another hazy future. But as I was lining up to help load supplies for another ship's journey, the slave master accidentally dropped a papyrus scroll at my feet. It unrolled about halfway. I picked it up, studied it for a moment, and noticed that while it was written in Latin, the document, a ship's cargo manifest, was practically illegible.

The ship was to set sail the next morning.

As I handed the scroll to the slave master, a slave himself, I told him of the errors. For my effort, he punched me in the face for speaking unbidden. However, later that evening during our meager meal, I was summoned to his quarters and closely questioned about my literacy. The slave master, Tobias, was impressed and gave me the position of scribe.

Each ship's cargo manifest had two copies; one remained in the port's shipping office, the other sent along with the vessel to its destination. To make an impression in my new job I worked hard through the night, rewriting the poorly written shipping manifest, and creating another. I couldn't find the vessel's copy, but I had a good idea where it was. So, just before the sun started to peek over the mountains, I finished my task and went to find my boss. By then the docks were teeming with activity, and at first, I had difficulty locating him. Then I saw a man dressed in finery, attended by slaves and guards—the owner, no doubt—approaching Tobias to presumably examine the manifest and ensure his cargo list was accurate. Though the morning was crisp, Tobias was sweating with fear as he rummaged about in his leather satchel to present the owner with his faulty one. As he drew the scroll from the bag, I knew I had to do something. Shouting at the top of my lungs, "*Tobias, Tobias, this one, this one.*", I sprinted towards them like a madman. Somehow I made it past the guards, ran up to Tobias, grabbed the old papyrus, handed him *my* copy, bowed, mumbled an apology, and ran off.

The owner examined the new copy and yelped with delight at my neat and precise handwriting. Tobias laughed so hard with relief that he started to cry, and of course took complete credit for my effort. Later, I sought him out. My brother's ship had not yet sailed, so I brashly insisted that he approach my owner to purchase Matthias.

The next day my brother appeared by my side.

Tobias had one demand of me, though. I was to secretly teach him how to read and write, for he had been faking his ability for months and was terrified of being found out. I promised that I would keep his confidence. I found my boss to be a fast learner, and soon he was literate in his native language, Latin.

Mastery of Greek soon followed.

As I tutored my student, I learned that he had once been a farmer, and his family had been captured and sold as slaves by the barbarians. He never saw his wife, two sons, and two daughters ever again. He'd wormed his way into the Slave Master position by sheer guile and intimidation, and he built his reputation on the bloody backs of fellow slaves.

But I saw a different side of Tobias. The fierce, intimidating visage he showed the world hid a warm and caring man underneath. As time went by, we grew close, and after some time, Tobias became almost a father to Matthias and me.

We worked hard to make our boss successful. Early on, and despite what he told us, Matthias and I had found that treating our fellow slaves well almost always resulted in better effort and output. Our success pleased the master; Tobias got promoted to Overseer. As he rose in importance, he brought my brother and me with him.

One day I asked Tobias whatever had happened to the rest of my family. He said he'd look into the matter. It took three junior scribes weeks to track them down. Eventually, Tobias told me the sad news that the sheep trader had sold my sisters to an Egyptian prince and they went with him back to Alexandria. In the next breath, my boss said the merchant had found my mother too sour-tempered and sold her to a low-level government official in the next town. Immediately I asked him if he could buy her.

Tobias laughed and said he was already making inquiries.

A week later, my mother joined us, and our reunion was joyous. It wasn't more than six months before Tobias asked the master for permission to marry my mother, for she was quick of wit, pleasing to the eye, and recognized Tobias's rising importance. The master permitted them to wed, and soon I was to be a big brother again.

A few months before my mother was to give birth, the master shocked us by announcing I had been sold to a prominent member of the Jewish Sanhedrin to pay off some gambling debts.

Worse yet, I was to live far away, in Jerusalem.

Devastated, I obeyed my master. I packed up my belongings, said my sad farewells, and joined my new owner, Nicodemus, on his ship.

When we were underway, Nicodemus summoned me to his cabin. I was a valuable slave, he said, and he expected me to work just as hard for him as I had my former master. Then he motioned me to sit at his table, poured himself a glass of wine, and spread out a papyrus roll on the surface. The papyrus showed a representation of the temple in Jerusalem. I was to memorize the layout. Then he said I was to keep the temple, its various courts, and surrounding areas clean, stocked, and profitable by purchasing the necessary ceremonial items sold for ritual use. I would also run his entire household, including his many businesses.

It was an enormous job. I knew nothing about any of my new duties and told Nicodemus so. With an icy look in his eye, he said I had better be a fast learner.

And I was.

By my fourth month on the job, I had introduced several new ways of organizing the army of slaves who worked tirelessly to keep the courts, and I soon learned Hebrew.

By the end of my third year, I was named Chief Slave Overseer.

By the end of my fifth year, I had proven my loyalty, so the Council of the Sanhedrin introduced me to the inner rooms and secret passages within the temple walls. Not the chamber containing the Holy of Holies. That was only for a chosen priest, once per year. As only the Sanhedrin and its trusted slaves knew, a maze of secret passages existed within and underneath the temple walls. The priests could walk from one end of the courtyard to the next, unobserved. Viewing ports were carved in the limestone walls too—cleverly constructed to allow the viewer to observe and listen to conversations in the courtyard without being seen.

I found great humor in the fact that the walls of the Women's Court had far more viewing ports than the rest of the temple grounds.

During my sixth year in Jerusalem, I had in mind to ask Nicodemus for permission to wed a fellow slave, Cassandra.

My beloved was in charge of his kitchens. One bright morning I approached him with our petition.

Nicodemus flatly denied our request and threatened to sell Cassandra. He angrily reminded me that we were slaves and that we were but property. I was overwhelmed.

The next day we had our Jesus moment.

At a little after sunrise, my crews were busy clearing away the previous day's dust and trash. I was inside the wall of the Women's Court, cleaning the passageway. I noticed Jesus of Nazareth teaching a group of merchants and travelers. Slaves from my master's house were forbidden to listen to the traveling preacher. But I was angry and feeling a bit rebellious.

I decided to eavesdrop.

Jesus was saying that people should not be hypocrites and commit the same sin they accuse others of doing. Then a group of Pharisees and Sanhedrin approached Jesus. I could see my master, Nicodemus, leading the assemblage. In tow was a naked woman clutching a small cloth below her waist. She had a cut over her brow and a swollen lip; smeared rivulets of blood ran down to her bosoms. She tried to cover herself modestly but was unsuccessful, for they were ample and well-formed.

The teachers of the law and the Pharisees listened until Jesus concluded his sermon. Then they pushed the woman to the front of the crowd, saying that the woman, caught in the very act of adultery, required justice. They loudly asked Jesus if it were proper to punish her by stoning her to death. The Law of Moses demanded it, they said.

Stone her.

As the woman wept softly behind him, Jesus cocked his head to the side and looked down at the ground as if he were contemplating the question. The crowd kept asking if she were to be stoned. Some rabble-rouser in the back tossed a rock in her direction, no doubt to press the point, but it landed ineffectually and was ignored.

Jesus slowly surveyed the group, and a hush fell over the entire Women's Court.

Although there were many people present, he met each person's eye; on some, he lingered for a few moments.

Jesus bent down and with his right index finger, started writing in the dust. From my vantage point in the wall, looking down, I could see everything he wrote.

He stood and surveyed the crowd. "Let any one of you who is without sin be the first to throw a stone at her." Then he bent down again and resumed writing. One by one the Sanhedrin, Pharisees and even those he was teaching in the court turned away and left. Soon only the woman and Jesus were there.

And me, unobserved.

Jesus stood. "Woman, where are they? Has no one condemned you?"

She slowly lifted her head and met his eyes. "No one, sir."

"Then neither do I condemn you," Jesus declared. "Go now and leave your life of sin."

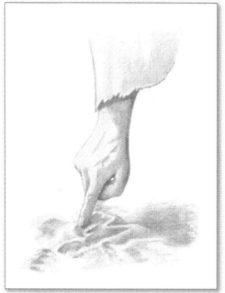

Then Jesus was alone. In front of him, dozens of melon and fist-sized stones littered the yard. He turned to face me, hidden in the wall. How the preacher knew I was there, I have no idea. He asked me what my heart's desire was; I replied, through the stone, that I wanted to marry Cassandra.

He smiled and told me to go and seek my master. As he slowly walked away, a gentle but persistent breeze eddied through the court, at first obscuring, then finally obliterating the writing in the dust.

When I got home, my master and Cassandra were waiting in his chambers for me. Ordinarily harsh and calculating, Nicodemus's countenance was warm, quiet and reserved. "I've reconsidered your request, Caleb. You have my blessing to wed, and I shall pay for your ceremony. May your union produce many children."

This Jesus had had a life-changing effect on him.

Completely taken aback, we could only offer our thanks and forgiveness. Things would be different, he said. And they were. Eventually, he became a follower of The Way, as did his entire household.

You are probably wondering what Jesus wrote in the dust that day. When I started listening to him from my hidden vantage point, Jesus was teaching that we should not to be hypocrites. Some have speculated that he listed the sins of each person present.

Well, you could be right, or you could be wrong.

I shall never tell, for as my darling wife, Cassandra, often reminds me when our twin sons Matthias and Tobias squabble, love covers a multitude of sins.

The End

The secret of contentment is knowing how to enjoy what you have and be able to lose all desire for things beyond your reach.

Two Denarii

A week ago, I, Pazel, the second eldest son, dined with my parents and their guests in our seaside home. There I spoke with a man from Jerusalem about Jesus of Nazareth. The traveling preacher was creating quite a stir in Judea, he said, by healing the sick, restoring sight, and performing other miracles. But I was taken aback when he made the fantastic statement that Jesus might even be the Messiah. I questioned him closely throughout the evening. Two other guests joined in to support his argument, and I was persuaded to meet and interview this Jesus myself.

I remembered the old saying, "If you want to go fast, go alone. If you want to go far, go together," so I packed some provisions on my trusted horse and set off, despite dire warnings from my uncle Ner about the dangers of going by myself.

"I am the rebel son of our family, an enigma to all, Ner," I grinned. "Be reasonable, uncle. Adventure is my middle name." He shook his head sadly and said that one day my headstrong ways will be my downfall. But as usual, I detected a bit of envy, for Ner was twelve years older, married, and had seven children. I was twenty-five and had no wife yet to slow me down. I wanted to wring the very last drop of living out of life before I married.

But I'm no fool. Despite being a semi-practicing Jew, I'm also a skilled and seasoned fighter, having spent four years abroad as a mercenary. I've learned the military tactics of many nations and become an expert with the sword, lance, and bow. I'm also skilled in hand to hand combat. Yet my secret weapon is that I learned to listen to my 'inner voice' that warns me when something is amiss.

I arrived in Jerusalem after a day's travel, and it took another day and a half to locate the traveling preacher.

I found his group seeking the shelter of a small thicket of trees, for the day was suffocatingly hot. Ominous dark clouds billowing over the mountains threatened rain.

I dismounted and paused for a moment, quickly figuring out who this Jesus was when he cured a leper of his disease. The man went away singing and praising God. Another man blessed Jesus for making his daughter walk again. Without even observing the customary greetings, I approached and cried out, "Good teacher, what must I do to inherit eternal life?"

Jesus smiled, and I felt welcome in his presence.

He bade me sit with others already in attendance, and his disciples made me wait my turn for his attention. I listened for a long while, and I liked what I heard. Then it was my turn, and I repeated my question. At first, his answer that I keep the commandments made my heart leap for joy, for I had done these since I was a small boy.

Eternal life seemed well within reach, and I had the world in the palm of my hand.

Then Jesus told me to sell my possessions, give them to the poor, then follow him. I was taken aback. This would radically change my life, for my family had amassed great wealth in land, livestock, slaves, and timber. I was to inherit these, so I turned away, sad.

As I mounted my horse, I heard him raise his voice to the crowd, "How hard is it for a rich man to enter the kingdom of heaven." Riding away, I realized his words were meant for my ears and understood I was making my choice.

I really, *really* like being wealthy.

I continued on to a cousin's house in Jerusalem, where I stayed for several weeks. One evening, while in the souk buying my dinner, I ran across an old comrade-in-arms, Nour, whom I had fought alongside in many clashes. We had saved each other's life several times and were close as brothers. I invited Nour to my cousin's home, where we reminisced over a sumptuous meal and Jerusalem's best wine. I learned that he had become a wheat farmer and lived quietly with his family in Jericho. Nour said parts of the ruined town were still discernable and invited me to join him as his guest to tour the remnants.

Jericho is the site of the ancient battle where the prophet Joshua once defeated the city by marching around it, shouting, and blowing horns. My warrior mind was intrigued, and of course, I accepted.

In preparation for my stay in Nour's home, I purchased beautiful gifts for his wife and children. I also outfitted myself in Judea's most elegant linen robes and outerwear, befitting my wealth and status.

Five days later, we set out for Jericho, some fifteen miles to the east as the crow flies. Unfortunately, crows fly in straight lines. The traditional road was full of switchbacks and curves which roughly tripled the distance. And, it was notoriously infested with thieves and robbers, something that travelers usually overcame by traveling in large groups.

Before we left, Nour produced two deadly Egyptian khopeshes, sickle-shaped swords, that resemble an animal's foreleg. We grinned with remembering how we had wielded such marvelous weapons in combat. These we concealed within easy reach.

About two hours into our journey, my companion pointed out a little-used short cut that he said would save us about nine hours and many miles. The alternative route would take us up a long, narrow trail on the sheer side of a cliff and down across a nondescript valley with a dry riverbed in the middle. The drop to our right side was several hundred feet straight down.

The heat was becoming increasingly oppressive, *and* we were men—so of course, we chose the more dangerous but shorter route. We noted, with some apprehension, darkening clouds high up in the mountains the direction we were traveling. My nagging 'inner voice' kept reminding me of the strong likelihood of a flash flood, and I mentioned this to Nour. He said he felt the same and would be happy when we reached the trail on the far side.

We continued on, not even talking much, for the hot desert air had shriveled our tongues.

At the peak of the climb, we spotted a band of about thirty thieves on the opposite side of the valley. Headed west and away, it appeared that they hadn't seen us. Then our cliffside path took a sharp turn to the left, which took us out of sight of the bandits. An hour later, when the trail straightened out, they were gone.

We sped up a little anyway.

When we finally reached the valley floor, it proved to have a steeper bank on the far side than Nour remembered. We explored a bit up and downstream with no success. Suddenly, our horses began acting skittish, and my 'inner voice' started screaming that something wasn't right.

Alarmed, I yelled to Nour that we needed to turn around and go back up the trail we had just descended to a widening in the path some fifty feet in elevation. The creators of the trail had carved out a turnout there so travelers coming from opposite directions could pass each other.

When we turned, our horses pulled *us* back up the trail.

Not long after we had reached our turnout, a thirty-foot wall of brown, foamy water laden with dead trees and brush, came roaring down the valley. Shocked and trembling with awe at the power of the water, we watched the tumult below. A few minutes later, to our disbelieving eyes, a wild-eyed camel somehow straddling a large tree trunk floated past us to an uncertain future.

Nour was the first to find his voice, "I haven't been this way for a few years, Pazel. Floods must have carved the opposite bank and made it taller. Another few minutes searching in the valley and we would have been washed away. You saved my life again."

Watching the torrent, I laughed with the giddy but numb relief that only cheating certain death brings. "Then our tally is nearly even, Nour."

With night falling, we decided to make camp on the trail and wait out the flood, which was already starting to recede. Nour tended the horses, and for security, I blocked the path further up the cliff face with some logs I brought up from the river. We ate our evening repast cold, for building a warming fire in such an exposed position would have brought unwanted attention.

I stood the first watch. Nour relieved me around midnight, but the night passed quietly.

The sun's first rays revealed a remarkable sight. The riverbed had been scoured clean as if the flood had never happened, and we could clearly see easy access up the far bank to the trail above.

Without even pausing for breakfast, we packed the horses and got underway.

We pushed hard for an hour and found the intersection of our trail and the main road to Jericho. We paused for a brief meal and to rest under a rocky, shady outcropping.

Right decision, lousy location.

In the middle of eating, a group of bandits attacked. We fought valiantly despite four to one odds. One of the men snuck up on Nour from behind and stuck a dagger high in his back. Instead of dying right away, Nour turned, beat his attacker senseless, and killed another who got too close. Then a rock found his head, and he collapsed on the sand.

I slowly backed up a small slope. With my back to higher ground, I fought like a madman, killing two. Ultimately, a stone thrown from the side brought me down. I do, though, dimly remember one of the attackers being called 'Barabbas.'

I regained consciousness after some time, woozy, lacerated, bloody, bruised, and naked. Our horses and my expensive linen garments were gone. Nour's body was nowhere to be seen. I managed to stagger to the road, then despite the sun being high in the sky, darkness took me.

Four days later I awoke in an inn. I was wrapped in rough bandages, desperately thirsty, and sick to my stomach. My head pounded with pain, and my eyes were swollen almost shut. The innkeeper's wife placed a damp cloth over my forehead and gave me sips of water. I drifted back into an uneasy sleep as the fog of confusion remained in my head.

Several more days passed until I could form words, and even more until I could hold a conversation. I learned that a Samaritan man, Abdiel, had found my body on the road, and brought me here. I was surprised because Jews and Samaritans customarily had nothing to do with each other. My rescuer had wrapped my wounds in cloths, then poured oil and wine on them to keep infection away. I arrived on his donkey, the innkeeper said, and the Samaritan had him given two silver denarii, about two months wages, for my care.

Abdiel said that he would be back to reimburse the innkeeper any additional expenses.

I was stunned. Compassion had come upon me from the most unlikely of places, and I was grateful beyond words. I resolved to find this Abdiel and thank him for his kindness.

Eight days later, as soon as I was able to walk without falling down, I started for Jericho and Nour's home. I needed to be the one to tell his wife what had happened.

The innkeeper had given me some greasy old garments, a worn pair of sandals, a straw hat, and provisions enough to reach Jericho. Because I was still fragile, he gave me his battered old donkey, Nebuchadnezzar, to ride and carry my gear. I looked like a pauper, was treated like a pauper, *was* a pauper.

For the first time in my life, I experienced the desperate ugliness of being poor.

I was terrified of being robbed again and dying alone. For protection, I petitioned to join a group of travelers heading in my  direction. Initially, they refused, but I slowly, painfully, got down on my knees. With tears in my eyes, I begged for mercy. One man called me 'pathetic,' another man, 'disgusting,' but in the end they pitied me, and I fell in at the rear of their column.

I couldn't keep up. Early on the second day, they left me. I suspect the leader of the group maintained a faster than usual pace to achieve this. But, because of my appearance, no one, not even a large group of bandits who passed going west, gave me a second glance.

I hated my poverty, but at the same time loved my poverty. Life is funny sometimes, yes?

Eventually, I crested a small hill, and Jericho lay in front of me.

Nour's farm was in the southern part of the city, and his property was easy to find. When I hailed the house from afar, to my astonishment, Nour came out to see who approached. He was covered with bandages too, and our celebration at seeing each other alive was tempered by not wanting to tear open our wounds. I learned that he also had been thought dead by the bandits. Instead, Nour had clung to life and staggered out into the desert looking for me. Shepherds found him hours later barely alive and nursed him to health. By the time he had recovered enough to search for me, I was gone, having been rescued by Abdiel the Samaritan.

I spent four months at Nour's home as we slowly regained our health. Honestly, I lingered a few months longer than necessary, for I had become enamored with—and ultimately betrothed to—the lovely Bina, his younger sister.

I sent word back to my family that I was safe. My parents, who assumed me dead, were overjoyed I was alive. They were also relieved that their rebel son had finally taken a wife and would be settling down.

One day, news came from Jerusalem that two anarchists, one named Barabbas, had been captured by the Romans during a robbery on the Jericho road. Both men faced the consequences of their efforts to overthrow the Roman rule: crucifixion. Nour and I remembered the name 'Barabbas' and felt vindicated. "Sow the wind, reap the whirlwind," said Nour, and I agreed.

After returning to my parent's home and marrying Bina, I found Abdiel after a brief search in Samaria. I thanked him for his kindness, repaid his denarii a hundredfold, and am now 'Uncle Pazel' to his many children. We visit each other's families often and have found that by simply respecting each other's beliefs, we can be friends despite what our cultures tell us.

Well, that's my story about meeting this Jesus of Nazareth. One day, for amusement perhaps, I'll seek him again and see if he still wants me to sell all my possessions. Despite what he says, though, in my heart I know I won't do it.

I really, *really* like being wealthy.

The End

Habit is a man's best friend or his worst enemy.

The Last Helper

Weak from blood loss, reeling from the cruel scourging and beatings at the hands of Roman soldiers, Jesus of Nazareth staggered up the street toward me. Over his shoulder, he dragged the top timber of his cross. With each agonized step, I expected him to collapse, and for a soldiers' spear to put him out of his misery—not that his death was that far off. Yet as he neared, the look on his battered face made no sense to me. This man was *determined* to reach Golgotha, the place of the skull, where he would be crucified until dead.

If he made it that far.

My business was spice trading, and over the decades I've traveled the world in search of its finest. While my body had become increasingly achy and my beard had long been grey, the exuberance of my youth surfaced yesterday when I spoke with some fellow traders fresh from Judea. Rumor had it, they said, that nine large caravans from the far east were to arrive in Jerusalem in two months.

I had to investigate.

I went to Selena, my wife, "Just one more trip before I die." She saw the wanderlust in my eyes, but I saw the serious look in hers. "You are old, Simon. And what of your wound? You do not heal as you did when you were a young man." Two days before, a camel had bitten my forearm just above my right wrist, almost to my elbow. It was quite painful too, but though it still seeped blood through the bandages, it *was* stitched up nicely, and I was no stranger to pain. I shrugged. "I will be fine, dear wife. Rufus and Alexander will take care of me."

She shrugged too, and we hugged. "Yes, they will. Our sons are competent young men. Then safe travels, beloved Simon. And bring me something exotic, please."

Four days later we joined other travelers from Libya headed east. The route from our home in Cyrene took us across the top of Africa, through the cities of Tobruk, Alexandria, and Cairo. During the first day's communal evening meal, one of the men from another group said that we might wish to use a more extended but lesser taken route to Alexandria, for thieves and barbarians had become common on the shorter road. I countered that I had heard the same, but the long way was over treacherous mountainous terrain and skirted the Sahara. After considerable debate, we chose the longer route. Alas, the decision was ill-fated; a rock slide carried away a donkey, and two of our slaves. When we arrived in Alexandria, Rufus bought another donkey and two slaves, sisters, to replace them. I laughed and questioned his wisdom of buying women, for the journey ahead was arduous, but he said they could read and write three languages. That they were fair and quite pleasing to the eye was but a coincidence, he said, and we could sell them in Jerusalem if we so desired.

Two days after we had arrived in Jerusalem, we sold the two female slaves he'd acquired in Alexandria. The buyer, the chief slave overseer of a rich Pharisee named Nicodemus, didn't hesitate when we asked a ridiculous price for each. After the transaction was complete, the new owner embraced the slave girls, who hugged him back and squealed with joy. I studied the girls and the overseer—and noticed a strong resemblance in their faces.

A week later we found the owners of the caravans and observed the customary rituals for a few days. The next morning, we got to examine their wares. To my disappointment, most of their goods were not what I was looking for; but after Alexander bought an exquisite golden tiger the size of his hand, and I some exotic cardamom, one of the merchants, Elon, took me aside and said a tenth caravan had arrived late last night. He offered for us to accompany them and view their treasures as they opened the packs, stored in a building not far away. This was a rare honor, and as we made our way towards what I hoped would be why we journeyed to Jerusalem, the streets began to thicken with an angry mob. Our hosts explained that a preacher, Jesus of Nazareth, was to be crucified for claiming to be king of the Jews and that this was his death procession to Golgotha. Hoping to flank the throngs of angry people, we detoured towards the Praetorium of Pilate.

Things didn't work out that well.

The crowd that lined both sides of the street had worshiped Jesus as king of the Jews only days before were now cursing him. The man next to me was screaming, "Set yourself free, Jesus." Another shouted, "How does it feel to be the king of the Jews?"

I was confused. Jesus's reputation was compassion and love for others, and several times I had spoken with men who insisted he had done nothing wrong.

Then Jesus crumpled, and the crossbeam, smeared with his blood, and bits of his flesh, rolled in my direction.

Much to my dismay, it stopped directly in front of me.

A hush fell over the crowd as Jesus lay in a heap. A soldier kicked him in the ribs, eliciting a moan, then the mob started up again. "Get up, king." I heard a woman cackle, "He saves others, but he cannot save himself."

And much worse.

A soldier grabbed my arm and dragged me out into the street, snarling, "Help the prisoner."

For a moment I resisted and felt a hot blaze of pain as stitches tore and my wound reopened. Though I'm robust and battle-tested, the razor tip of the soldier's sword appeared at my throat, and I thought it wise to give in.

I helped Jesus to his feet, then picked up the timber. My wound was in flood stage, slicking my robe, then mingling with his. The crosspiece was weighty, about one hundred pounds, but no match for my brawn. Jesus put his hand on my other shoulder for support, and said hoarsely, "Thank you, friend."

I took a moment to study him. How he was still standing, I did not know. Lash wounds covered almost all of his exposed skin; in many places bone and sinew showed. His cheeks were raw, for his beard had been yanked out. His hair was a bloody mat, and a crown of bramble thorns still rode on his head.

His split lips, mashed nose, and two broken teeth bore witness to the savagery of his beating. Too, there were abrasions, cuts, blood, and dirt all over his face. All I could manage was, "You're welcome, sir." Then the crowd found their voices and a soldier pushed us forward.

We had some two or three hundred yards up a slight incline to go. Jesus fell a second time, and as the soldiers let him catch his breath, a woman offered him some water. Another woman wiped his face. A third touched his brow, tears in her eyes. A brave man yelled encouragement. I resolved to remember and cherish their kindness amid such horror. He laid there for a long while, almost two minutes. I thought him dead.

Again, a soldier's prodding urged him—and me—on.

I helped Jesus to his feet, and for the first time, he saw Golgotha. His breathing, dry and raspy, quickened as strength flowed from some deep reservoir. We stood together, brothers in this struggle, and I found my voice. "I'm sorry, Jesus. I truly am."

He managed a grimace, "I thank you, friend."

As we continued towards Golgotha, Jesus passed his mother and some of his friends. Their interaction was heart-wrenching, and I found tears in my eyes. Then, a bit further on, he fell for the third time. I think even the hardened Roman guards were impressed with Jesus's resolve, for this time they allowed him to lay quietly for a few moments. His breath came in heaving gasps now. Soft, dark scabs were forming on some of his lacerations, but the deeper ones still bled. I helped him up; we made our way to the end of the road. Golgotha.

His end of the road.

As the soldiers led him away, Elon rushed to my side and took us to his home nearby. Our hosts were appalled at the soldier's treatment of me and said my kind-heartedness towards a condemned man said a lot about my character. Smeared with Jesus's and my blood. I wanted nothing more than to bathe and tend to my arm. But too, I needed to visit Golgotha and say farewell to the man who impressed me so. I knew little of his philosophy or the circumstances that had crossed our paths, but I felt compelled to see him on his cross. I wanted to know more about him, and why he seemed so determined to be crucified.

Alexander had purchased a new robe for me during my slow, arduous walk with Jesus. With the help of servants who scrubbed the dried blood from my skin, I was soon my old self. I was disappointed to find most of the stitches on my arm had torn free, and, after Rufus took special care to bathe my camel bite with a weak vinegar solution, a servant sewed up my wound.

I asked Elon and his friends to indulge me with a detour to see Jesus, and they agreed. When we arrived, he had already been stripped naked and was hanging from the cross. A sign over his head read, "King of the Jews." The head of the Roman garrison, Centurion, came over to us and asked about my arm. I asked him about Jesus, and about how he came to be hanging there. To my surprise, he seemed unsettled and

distracted. We spoke for a few moments; then his duties took him elsewhere.

I stood in front of Jesus. Even though speaking caused him horrible pain, he managed, "Thank you, friend."

When I turned away, I had tears in my eyes.

We made our way to the building where the tenth caravan's wares were stored. Eighteen camels and twenty-three donkeys had carried it over a great distance. Although they mostly knew what to expect, our hosts hadn't seen its contents. As they opened each package, we gasped with wonder and excitement. Gold, diamonds, spices, silks, exotic foods, tea, and, to my surprise, a small amount of opium were now in front of us. Elon offered a bit of the narcotic to dull my pain, but I declined, for I wanted to be in full control of my faculties. Instead, I chose a glass of robust wine and chewed some white willow bark for its painkilling properties.

I bought a beautiful sari for Selena and a bolt of turquoise silk. To my delight, I found a new variety of saffron, and, what our hosts described as whale excreta, musky ambergris.

Time flew by, and we broke for a late lunch just before three o'clock. As we stepped outside, to our alarm, the sky had darkened almost like night, and the winds had picked up. Then a tremendous earthquake rocked Jerusalem and knocked us off our feet. Fortunately, our building was unharmed, but we could see the damage up and down the street. Elon set guards, locked his shop, and we rendered aid as best we could to those injured in the quake.

I spoke with some of Jesus's followers over the next eleven days. They said he walked on water, healed people, cast out demons and even raised a youth from the dead. They said Jesus had claimed to be the Son of God, had conquered death and now lived again. I laughed and said how could this be, but they said Jesus had appeared to them. They said Jesus died in fulfillment of scripture, and showed me in the holy book where all this was prophesized hundreds of years before.

It made sense to me, and finally, I understood his drive to reach Golgotha.

So now we are almost home, our packs laden with goods from Jerusalem and the far east. As for me, I often think about Jesus's crucifixion and our chance meeting on that street. My bite wound has finally healed, in the curious shape of a cross.

The cross of Jesus, my brother in the struggle.

The End

The smallest good deed is better
than the grandest intention.

Right Hand Man

My horror grew as I watched as the Roman military machine going about its business of preparing two other men and me for crucifixion. Then I heard cursing in Latin, one of three languages I speak, and found dark humor despite my predicament. I was minutes away from being hung on the cross until dead, and some idiot had forgotten to bring the iron nails they would drive through my hands and feet into the wood.

The Centurion dispatched two soldiers to the guardhouse, who returned all too soon.

The Roman guard's stinking breath caused me to gag as he grunted and yanked my right arm up and away from my body. Although I was determined not to show any pain, I cried out as something tore hotly deep within my shoulder.

He guffawed wetly, choking on his phlegm. When he caught his breath, he bent down and spat in my face. He growled in broken Aramaic, "Hurts? Good. I kill you, Abel. My name is Latus in Latin, but Cain in Hebrew. Like the Jews believe. Cain and Abel. You know the Jews? I ask for to kill you. For humor. But you tell me about your terrorist friends; I hurt you less."

Then he looped a thick hempen rope, dark and crusty with the dried blood of others, around my wrist and started to tie it to the timber.

I groaned loudly. In Latin, I said to Cain, "Hurt less? Yes. Come closer. I will tell you about the others in my group." His eyes widened, and he knelt on one knee close to my face.

With all the spittle I could muster, I spat into his face and laughed. "Take that, you son of a Roman pig."

The crushing punches and kicks to my head and torso seemed never-ending; my world swirled, and I detached from my body, uncomprehending. Idly, I wondered how I got to be where I was.

Oh yeah, I remember: I was a thief who became an anarchist murderer.

Let me explain. My name is Abel, and I stole from people who live in the slums. Firewood, tools left unattended, dirty pots and pans, and even strips of leather were easy pickings. Young children were my favorite victims. They seldom made a sound when I pried a morsel of food from their grubby little fingers, for the silent snarl on my face usually shut them up. I worked cities along the Mediterranean, staying in one village long enough to make a few quick scores then moving on.

My life of petty theft changed the day a group of women accused me of stealing their undergarments that were drying on the riverbank. As I professed my innocence, a small boy discovered where I'd cached their property. The women raised such an outcry that a contingent of passing Roman soldiers decided to investigate.

I ran.

Their sergeant ordered me to halt, but I fled anyway and soon outdistanced the guards, who were hindered by their armor and shields. The penalty for theft was severe, and I was already a repeat offender, so I ran for my life. I knew the soldiers would not stop looking for me, so I ran for almost an hour along a narrow sheep path deep into the mountains. Exhausted, I threw myself into a thick copse of juniper trees and discovered the oblong mouth of a cave at my feet.

I hate caves. They're the place of demons, monsters, and madness, but having to choose between real and imagined death, well, I'm a skinny man, and I squeezed in.

The afternoon's light struggled to penetrate; I inched down its sloping floor into the dimness with caution. I caught a whiff of pungent animal urine and something fetid and foul, a leopard's kill perhaps, and I hoped it was out hunting. Then I could hear the guards calling to each other, but eventually, their noises grew faint and stopped.

As the sun was setting, I resigned myself to a night underground.

Just before twilight passed into night, I went outside and gathered some brush from just outside the cave mouth, enough for several hours of heat and light. I also found a pine that had recently lost a limb and collected a fist-sized chunk of sticky sap, perfect fuel for a makeshift torch. Back in the cave, I rubbed my firestone rapidly on a small, flat, dry branch, then added kindling to birth a tiny flame. I soon had a small fire.

I smoothed the soil and lay on my back. The ceiling was dark with soot; humans had taken shelter here before. Hoping they might have left something of value, I mounted the pine sap on a stick, ignited it, and explored deeper into my new home. A jumble of rags turned out to be a shrunken, half-eaten corpse lying on its side twenty-five feet further back into the cave. I shrieked, dropped my torch and scrambled back to my fire. I threw branches on it and lit up the entire cavern. When my hands stopped shaking, thankful that no monster or demon had attacked, I gathered my courage and went back to look at the body. It was a man, and the cave's dry air had shrunken and partially mummified his body -- which to my relief, hadn't been eaten after all. The shaft of an arrow protruded from his back. When I tried to remove the projectile, his head fell off and rolled several feet. Horrified, I threw myself away from the corpse and retched.

Later, for the sake of my sanity, I scraped out a shallow grave, dragged him into it, reassembled his body, and buried the poor fellow. Although I hadn't practiced any religion since I was a boy, a burial prayer came to mind, and I recited it with an intensity that surprised me. I found his possessions, a cache of dried food, weak wine in a skin, bedding, and an exceptionally well-crafted Bedouin shabria dagger, near his body. Later, when my hunger and thirst overcame the corpse's faint, lingering odor, I found his food and wine satisfying. I drank deeply, and again until its pale purple sweetness spilled down my chin.

Belly full, I banked the coals of my fire and drifted off to an uneasy sleep.

Low voices and the sound of a snapping branch awakened me. I crab-crawled almost to the cave mouth where I could see light, yet the faint chirping of crickets told me it was still night. Several men holding torches were facing the cave, and two were preparing to crawl inside.

I spoke from the cave, "Friends, I mean you no harm." One of the men on his hands and knees yelped and scrambled away. The others drew daggers.

I stifled a laugh. "I am not a ghost but a simple man who has taken shelter for the night. Here, let me come forth and let us speak. I mean no harm."

A baritone voice, quiet and used with authority, replied, "Come forth and be known."

I tucked the dagger into my waistband and wiggled out. In front of me were six rough looking men. I recognized one of them, a fellow thief, and saw the flicker of recognition in his eyes. He stepped forward, and we shook hands. "I know you. *Ahlan*, Abel."

Ahlan. The traditional informal Arabic greeting. If I were in trouble, he would have greeted me in a coldly formal way.

"Ahlan, Pilar. I am happy to see you." I hadn't seen him since he and I pickpocketed a crowd listening to the Jewish king Herod make a speech.

"Abel. What were you doing in that cave?"

"Running from the hated Romans. What else would drive me there? You know I hate caves."

Everyone laughed, and he introduced me to his companions. Then Barabbas, the leader of the group, asked about my dagger, and I told them about the corpse. As my lair was their destination, one by one we disappeared underground. The dead man in the cave was one of theirs, and I gained instant acceptance.

Pilar had joined a group of rebel criminals devoted to overthrowing the Roman rule, and Barabbas was its leader. We spoke long into the night, about how a Jewish king was supposed to rise, oust the Romans, and reinstate Jewish rule in Judea. This group wanted to support the rebellion.

Revolution.

I decided to join them. A Jewish king rising from the people and overthrowing the Roman rule? I was all for that. I swore allegiance to Barabbas and his movement. Using my dagger, I became a robber. During a robbery on the Jericho road, I became a murderer.

Seven months later the Romans caught Barabbas and me just outside of Jerusalem. I was beaten and imprisoned in the squalid Roman dungeon, in solitary confinement. I knew crucifixion was in my future. Nailed to a cross, I would suffer the cruelest death ever devised.

Some months later, the guards threw another prisoner into my cell. His name was John, and at first, I thought he was a lunatic because all he talked about was the coming Messiah—but that didn't matter—for I hadn't spoken to anyone for a long time. We talked for days; invariably the conversation turned to Jesus, the traveling preacher who taught love. John insisted that the holy man had healed the sick and even raised some people from the dead. My cellmate also claimed to have baptized Jesus. Inwardly I wondered, but I always replied to John's impassioned statements with, "Messiah? But are you *sure*, John?"

One evening, several weeks after John's arrival, palace guards entered our lockup, seized my cellmate, then beheaded him. They placed his head on a silver platter and whisked it away. A day later they came for his headless corpse.

Every few months another prisoner would join me in my cell; they always spoke of Jesus, the traveling preacher John claimed was the Son of God. Sadly, after a short stay, they were taken, whipped, and killed. My existence became the mindless repetition of a meager daily meal and weekly emptying of my bucket. Every day became night; every night had no hope. Days stretched into weeks; weeks into months. Rats and roaches became my companions, at least until hunger overcame my loneliness.

One morning, three years—maybe more—into my anguish, my door swung open.

It was my turn to die.

I was unconscious from Cain the guard's beating; the other guards had to throw a filthy bucket of water in my face to bring me back around. This time, they hammered the nails through my feet and hands then lifted me up to face the crowd. The pain was excruciating, and I struggled to breathe.

There were three of us hanging on our crosses in a semi-circle. Jesus, the preacher John had spoken about in our jail cell, was in the center. He had been beaten and whipped mercilessly; a crown of thorns ringed his head. A sign over his head read, 'King of the Jews.' To Jesus's left was another criminal, a thief like me. I was on Jesus's right.

A large crowd, sprinkled with both Pharisees and Sadducees in colorful robes, had gathered in front of us to witness the preacher's death.

My perception of time seemed to slow down, and I could see, hear and smell more acutely than ever before. I heard people in the crowd saying that Jesus had cured their sickness or had performed a miracle on their loved one. I saw one man insisting to a Centurion that Jesus had healed his withered hand. Another man, a boat captain from the Sea of Galilee, said Jesus had calmed a raging storm in his presence. A man and his wife added their story that Jesus had cast a demon from their daughter. Others told similar stories of healings and miracles.

Most of the people said all they had done was ask for Jesus's mercy. I was astounded. So many, from such different backgrounds couldn't be wrong.

The other man being crucified loudly condemned Jesus. Several people in the crowd jeered and mocked the preacher too, as did the guards. Some of the Jewish elite sneered at him, saying that if he indeed was God, he should bring himself down from the cross. I joined in for a little while, but then Jesus said in a loud voice, "Father forgive them, for they know not what they do."

I remembered my cellmate, John, insisting that Jesus was God's son. And I was ashamed.

When the sun was directly overhead, the sky darkened, and roiling currents of wind washed over us. The soldiers milled about in confusion, and Cain, the one who spat into my face, shook his fist at the heavens.

Despite my impending death, I had a spark of hope.

To my left, it was apparent that Jesus wouldn't last very long. Beaten, flogged almost to death, and now, hanging on the cross, Jesus leaked blood and ooze from practically every inch of his body.

I felt a strange connection with the preacher. When I considered the crowd's witness, Jesus's forgiveness of those who were killing him, darkness during mid-day, and John my cellmate's insistence that Jesus was the Son of God in human form, I was convinced.

The criminal on Jesus's left was heckling him, and I told him to stop. Then I said to Jesus, "Remember me when you enter your kingdom."

Jesus turned to me and said, "Truly I tell you, today you will be with me in paradise."

Soon after that, he died, and a great earthquake shook the city. The Centurion ordered the breaking of my and the other criminal's legs to hasten our deaths. Cain, the soldier, came to me with a sledgehammer. He spat at me again, roared with laughter, and swung it over his head in a whirling arc. "Abel, now my pleasure I kill you. Cain kills Abel again."

I screamed in agony as the bones in my left leg splintered. Then, somehow the pain subsided, and peace flooded my mind. As he prepared to break my right leg, I took a big breath, and said to him, "I am Abel. In a few moments, I shall be in paradise, as Jesus said, Cain."

My right leg snapped, my arms now supported my entire body's weight. Death was coming fast.

As darkness closed in, I managed to croak, "When you die, where will you go?"

The End

Let us realize that what happens round us is largely out of our control, but that the way we choose to react to it is inside our control.

Thief

My old friend Amos raised the wineskin, drank deeply, then stared at the pulsing reddish black coals in his hearth. A few drops clung to the jumbled white whiskers on his chin and glowed rubylike in the firelight. His voice, wheezy and wet, barely traveled to me. "That's good wine. Thank you for sharing, Barnabas. But now, tell me of how you came to seek refuge in my humble compound this cold night."

The familiar smells and the warmth of the room felt good after many months living in tents. My host handed me the wineskin and I, too, quenched my thirst. "Thank you for allowing my men and me to stay under your protection, Amos. We are on our way home from spice trading in distant lands, and we are here seeking shelter because a snowstorm in the mountain passes to the west had to be waited out."

I paused. "And, old friend, in all honesty, I wanted to ask you about Judas Iscariot, betrayer of Jesus, for I have always been curious. You knew him well. What can you tell me?"

For a few minutes he closed his eyes, and his breathing grew deep and regular. I thought he might have fallen asleep, and I cleared my throat gently.

Amos chuckled, opened his eyes, and this time his voice was firm. "No, not asleep, Barnabas, just remembering. You must understand, that I was close with Judas early in life, like brothers. We told each other our deepest secrets, things that we would keep even from our real family. Yes, I knew he was a thief. Yes, I was also a thief then, but I put that aside as we grew up. I grew disgusted by what he became and tried to distance myself from him. But Judas always sought me out and unburdened himself, especially the night he betrayed Jesus. He wasn't the smug, selfish criminal I knew. Somehow, he was both Judas *and* something awful, full of evil and wickedness. I was afraid, but I think *he* was terrified. And though he wanted to talk, I think he really wanted to be reassured he was still human."

My host stood, laid another branch on the cooling embers, and poked it with a long stick. A swirl of sparks rose, then the fire flared as lesser twigs caught.

With an intensity that surprised me, Amos continued, "I recoiled at his appearance that night. But what could I do, Barnabas? Turn Judas Iscariot away? Even a monster needs someone to talk to."

Suddenly, the main branch ignited and flooded the room with its warm glow. I could see tears flowing down my friend's cheeks, and I was moved.

"Barnabas, did you know Judas left me letters he wrote to himself? He said he poured out his soul in them." Amos stood and shuffled into another room, returning with a crudely built cedar box. He put it next to my feet, turned and spat into the flames. "Judas left me *this*. His essence is captured here. I am illiterate, and though I *want* to learn to read, I deliberately kept myself that way so I would not be tempted to soil *my* soul with *his* words. Many, many times I wanted to cast the box into the fire and free myself of him, but for some reason, I never could. Barnabas, take this box of Judas's soul. I never want to see it again."

Our talk turned to other things, and our conversation produced both lamentation and laughter. Then we turned in for the night. Morning brought bright blue skies in the mountains and my departure home.

In my possession was Judas's cedar box wrapped in a waterproof calfskin cover, and in Amos' hands a box of my most delicate spices from halfway around the world.

Eight days later I read the first entry from the man who betrayed Jesus of Nazareth.

Stolen honey cake in hand I tore through the alfalfa field with all the speed my thirteen-year-old legs could muster, but the Roman soldier behind gained with every step. Then, as I hurdled a low stone fence into a cow pasture, my sandal caught the top, and the sun-baked ground rose to meet me.

I saw stars.

Laughing, the guard grabbed the back of my tunic and threw me face first into an enormous pile of wet dung. More stars. He knelt on one knee, rolled me over, unsheathed his short sword, and smacked its flat side hard right between my

eyes. A white-hot bolt of pain filled my face as my nose flat-
tened, and my mouth filled with blood. In Aramaic, he asked
me if I was ready to die for being a thief. Gagging, I shook
my head no, but, through the blood, pain, and stench, said
defiantly that he wouldn't kill me, for my father was Simon, a
prominent Pharisee.

"Yeah?" His eyes narrowed, then he tore open my tunic and
carved SPQR, the emblem of the Roman Empire, into my chest.
I howled in pain.

"Pontius Pilate usually has thieves killed, boy. Even young,
arrogant brats like you, even with influential fathers like yours.
Next time you are caught stealing, my blade will taste your
heart. Understand? That little gift on your chest should remind
you all your life that you and your disgusting Jewish nation
of swine are the property of Rome." He stood and sheathed
his weapon. "And we will know you're a thief." With that, he
turned and trotted back to his fellow soldiers on patrol.

Eventually, the pain subsided. As I cursed the soldier, I
found a morsel of pastry in my still clenched fist, a small prize
which cost me a big price. As I chewed, the sweet honey mixed
with the coppery taste of blood in my mouth. And I liked it.

I gagged and put down the scroll. Was Judas a lunatic even
during childhood?

I kept reading.

Mama, using poultices and potions, managed to remove
the scar on my chest and almost restored my nose to its former
glory. She told me to forgive, but father told me to remember

that my nose came from the hated Romans. I think he was angrier with me that I was caught stealing, not that I pilfered in the first place. But the memory of it is forever seared into my mind, and I vowed that I, Judas Iscariot, would spend my life working towards seeing the Romans expelled from Judea, preferably by force.

There was more, much more. From an early age, his scrolls revealed him to be a conniving liar and master manipulator of people. As Judas entered adulthood, he had learned his numbers well enough to embezzle denarii from his employers. He funneled some of it to the underground movement to overthrow Rome, but most went into his personal accounts. Somehow, his treachery was never uncovered. It seems that he imagined himself to be smarter than everyone else.

Judas's mother and his fiancée died in a tragic house fire that also consumed his home next door. I was stunned to learn that to soothe his pain, he would walk the streets for hours after nightfall, often seeking out dark places where depravity was the norm. He later married and sired children, but his thirst for the sick and twisted never abated.

As I read, Judas's self-absorption gave way to searing anger over the occupying Romans when he repeatedly witnessed their brutality on his people. He then yielded to guarded excitement when he learned from the holy men in the temple that the coming Messiah was soon to lead the Jews in getting rid of Judea's invaders.

Judas continued,

Many say Jesus is to be our king. I must get closer to him and see if this is true. If so, he can significantly assist my comrades and me in our plans.

A few days later this entry:

Three days ago, I met the carpenter-turned-preacher from Nazareth. To my surprise, he asked me to become one of his closest disciples. I wisely accepted. Today, I watched him heal a woman of blindness and a child from being unable to speak. What kind of sorcery can this be, and, more importantly, how can I get him to lead us in our revolt? And how can I profit from it?

Then, because the other disciples were mostly simple fishermen unused to dealing with money, Judas was given responsibility for the purse.

At first, I handled the purse with honor, but after a few months, the sheer volume of money being donated for our support, and the untracked disbursements became overwhelming. Money was handed to me without hesitation, and I gave it out as asked, sometimes because the carpenter's son said to but other times because I was caught up in being kind and generous to the poor. But one day I was in the bazaar, and I saw honey cakes for sale, the same kind I had stolen as a young lad when the soldier caught me. I slipped three into my pocket, and the merchant just grinned. I realized then that because I was one of the twelve, I could do just about what I pleased. Later, when I first chewed the pastry, I could again taste the blood from my broken nose so long ago. My hatred for the Romans was rekindled into a white-hot inferno.

I read on, fascinated that Jesus had chosen such a wicked man to follow him. Over the next three years of Jesus's ministry, on many occasions, Judas Iscariot tried to get Jesus to commit to leading a rebellion but was always rebuffed. *Jesus dismisses talk of revolt. Instead, he talks about love, forgiveness, and the kingdom of heaven. I call such ideas filth, but the number of people falling for his filth increases every day. He is supposed to be king of the Jews, and I want him to lead the war against Rome. I want rebellion, hatred, and, above all, piles of dead Romans.*

When Jesus talks of love, I want to kick the dust at his feet and scream, 'what is love?' But of course, I dare not.

Then I, Barnabas, opened the last scroll. Judas had hatched a plot with the high priests of the Jews, the Sadducees, to betray Jesus to them. In Judas's twisted reasoning, once arrested, Jesus would announce himself as king of the Jews, rally the people around him, and overthrow the occupying Romans.

The Jewish priests angled for a different outcome. They wanted to kill Jesus for blasphemy, as he had claimed to be the Son of God on several occasions. The priests expected the Romans to quash the challenge to Rome's authority, by killing Jesus, the rebellion's leader.

Unmentioned was the alarming loss of incoming tithes and offering revenue coming into the Jewish temple—and the loss of control over the people because so many Jews had decided to follow Jesus.

Yet Judas Iscariot, that rodent of a man, believed the townspeople would protect Jesus from both the Romans and the priests—then, as king, lead the Jews to a successful overthrow of the hated Romans.

Caiaphas, the high priest, offered me thirty pieces of silver to bring Jesus to him, and I was insulted. That's the price of a common slave. Of course, I think Jesus is worth much more, but what price revolution? I took it anyway.

I was aghast. Judas had agreed to betray Jesus for money.

That day, I was greatly encouraged when Jesus entered Jerusalem, for the townspeople welcomed him as Messiah and king. That evening, we twelve disciples celebrated Passover with him in a donated room. During the meal, Jesus predicted that one of us disciples would betray him. Then Jesus dipped bread into a bowl of olive oil and handed it to me. He said, "What you are about to do, do quickly."

As I went out into the night, I had a deep feeling that something was about to go horribly wrong, and I was powerless to stop it.

I made my way to Caiaphas, and somehow, I felt worms start to gnaw on my soul.

That was the last entry Judas made in his letters. I was sickened.

Worms. Silver. A kiss.

When the sun rose the next morning, I went high up into the hills and built a small campfire to burn the scrolls, so the words of Judas Iscariot, betrayer of Jesus of Nazareth, would not soil my home. One by one, I slowly fed them into the fire, where hungry flames quickly devoured the dry parchments. Then I tossed the cedar box into the fire, and when it had turned to ash, from low and far away, I thought I heard a man's voice howling in agony.

Or perhaps it was just the wind.

A year later, just after nightfall, I again tapped on Amos's modest wooden door. Just like last time, a storm was brewing; the icy wind gripped my cloak, threw back my hood, and threatened to extinguish my oil lantern. But I persisted, and a moment later he opened the door a crack. When he recognized me, he welcomed me inside. Soon we were warming ourselves in front of his hearth. His wife served us dates and small cakes sweetened with honey, and it was my honor to produce a wineskin with wine from my presses.

Amos drank deeply, smacked his lips and complimented my vineyards. "And what brings you here, this winter's night, Barnabas? Are you venturing off to distant lands again?"

I shook my head. "No, I came here because I wanted to tell you, Amos. I *needed* to tell you. I burned the scrolls and the wooden box. The words of Judas the betrayer are no more."

Amos stared silently into the flames for several minutes. Finally, he stood, tossed a brushy piece of kindling into the hearth and walked into the other room. The fire flared as the twigs and wood ignited and the room was bathed in warm, yellow light.

When he returned, he brought an ornate acacia box and a small, low table. My host grunted as he set it before him in front of the fire and took out several scrolls.

He opened one and spread the parchment in front of him. I could see letters and numbers written in Hebrew, the language of our people.

He cleared his throat. I could see tears streaming down his cheeks. He brushed them away, but they were quickly replaced by more. Amos turned to me. "Yes, I am free of him, Barnabas, my friend. Thank you."

He studied the document. As his finger traced the words on the scroll, Amos read softly, "In the beginning, God created the heavens and the earth..."

The End

A man is not old until regrets take the place of dreams.

The Other Mary

I gently woke Mary Magdalene, our friend, and house guest. "Mary, it's almost light, we must tend to the Master's body." She stirred, yawned, and sat up. Tears were already forming in her eyes, and mine, for Jesus, our master—and my nephew—had been crucified on Friday, just two days before. Now, Sunday, the Sabbath was past, and we were going to tend to his body, laying in Joseph of Arimathea's tomb.

I had already stirred the coals in the hearth, warming our morning meal, though neither of us had much appetite. The night before, my husband, Cleopas, had warned me to be careful when we walked to the tomb in the early morning hours.

He shook his head. "Robbers and wild animals stir in the night, Miri. Wake me then, and I shall go with you."

Miri. I loved it when he called me by my nickname. "No, Opie, my dear husband, Mary Magdalene and I shall be all right. Jerusalem is still numb from the execution, and I really doubt we shall encounter any robbers or hungry bears."

He laughed sadly, softly. "I pity the man or beast that runs afoul of you two tomorrow morning, hungry or not."

My knee joint popped and woke my husband as I knelt on our bedstead's mattress to tenderly bid him farewell. Instead of emerging from slumber as he usually did, Cleopas was instantly awake. He sat up and grabbed my forearm. "Miri. Listen. I had a dream: a man in a white robe told me to tell you to take your staff to the tomb." I looked into his eyes and saw he was frightened for me. "You must take your staff with you. Please, do it for me." I kissed him on his forehead and said I would. We embraced, and he stepped out of bed. "I am getting up now also, to join the eleven where they are hidden. Meet me there for the noon meal."

I nodded. Final preparations of Jesus's body shouldn't take more than a few hours, for Nicodemus and others had already purchased most of the materials and started the process.

Mary and I left the house quietly. I was already planning my route from the tomb to the disciples' hideaway, past the best shops selling the choicest foodstuffs for the midday meal. When I removed the staff from its storage space above our front door, I realized that I hadn't thought about it for many years. Crafted by Jesus in his father's workshop, long before he started on his road to the cross, the straight, six-foot piece of fire-hardened acacia was the same wood Moses used for the Ark of the Covenant's poles so long ago. I remember the day Jesus gave it to me. Manhood was dawning on his skinny frame, and blond peach fuzz was sprouting on his upper lip. His voice squeaked as he urged me to take it. "Someday a piece of wood will save you, Aunt Miri." Jesus was so embarrassed about his voice and so earnest with his gift that I chuckled, commented favorably on his workmanship, and accepted the staff. I hadn't the heart to give it away—or burn it for heat— so I stored it above our door, and there it remained.

Until now.

Brightly burning oil lamps in hand, heavy satchels full of spices to anoint Jesus's body over our shoulders, we moved through the streets of Jerusalem. We passed four Roman army foot patrols; an officer slightly nodded his head in silent greeting. Here and there, merchants were setting up shop for the day, and though it was still dark, I could see the eastern sky beginning to brighten.

Mary Magdalene cleared her throat. "Pardon me if I am intruding, but I've always wanted to ask you and Cleopas about Jesus. He was your nephew. What was Jesus like as a boy? Was he the perfect child, always obedient and attentive to his parents?"

I stifled a laugh as memories of Jesus flooded my mind. "No, he was an ordinary boy, late to supper sometimes, forgetful at others. But I remember once visiting with his mother as Jesus was playing with some of his friends in the courtyard. Out the window, I saw him pick up a dead bird off the ground, and it flew away. Maybe it wasn't dead. I always

meant to ask him about that." We picked our way around
a collapsed structure's broken column from the earthquake
that struck right when Jesus died, and I remembered another
incident in Jesus's boyhood. "He spent a great deal of time
in his father's workshop, learning carpentry. Once, when he
was almost four, I was visiting, and Joseph sent him into the
house for a left-handed mallet. We had our fun with him that
time."

We both giggled, and for a moment our spirits lifted.

I continued, "He was a normal boy, but as a man, I saw
him cure a leper. Wholly cured. I saw Jesus minister to a donkey that had been attacked by a lion. The beast had a long,
deep wound on its neck and terrible bite marks on its flank.
Jesus's prayed over the animal, and it was healed. Healed.
I saw a man with a withered hand have his hand restored.
Healed. Then there was the water turned into wine at a wedding." We walked in silence for a few moments as we pon-
dered those and many other events. "I saw him bring back a
little girl from the dead." I felt a surge of pride in knowing
him as my nephew. "But, but...*how* did he do these things?"

"He cast demons from me too, Miri. Seven. Yes, how?
That's the word that doesn't make any sense. How?" Mary
Magdalene paused. "His teachings were remarkable too. We
are to love one another. Forgive one another, and so much
more. He understood the Torah, and at such a young age.
How did he have so much wisdom? And when Jesus started
teaching in the temple, the Pharisees and Sadducees began to
hate him, because he claimed to be fulfilling prophecy right
then. Later he claimed to be the Son of God, and that's why
they had him killed."

She paused, then continued, "I thought he was just kidding. But he never recanted, and never tried to save himself. Isn't that a little crazy? Was he a lunatic?"

I said firmly, "No. Jesus was the sanest man I ever met, but I cannot understand why he taught what he taught, and did what he did. Maybe he really is God's son. But that cannot be, because he's dead, and here we go to tend to his body. But how did he perform such miracles?" I shook my head. "*How*. It's all beyond me."

We walked together in silence for a few minutes.

"But, Mary, can I ask you a personal question? I've always wanted to ask, but there never seemed to be the right time." A thoughtful look on her face, she nodded.

"Jesus cast seven demons out of you. But before he did, well, what did it feel like and how did you come to be demon possessed?"

Her reply came slowly. "I didn't trust that God would sustain me. My business was in decline, and I sought out a woman who practices white magic to help me make more money. Actually, all magic is evil, but I didn't realize it at the time. Anyway, she lives on the outskirts of the city, and when I entered her home, I felt a chill wrap around my soul. We sat, she asked me what I wanted, took my gold and silver, then told me to invite a spirit into me to guide me. I did. Then things started to change. The best way I can explain it is that I was not myself. Now, I am Mary of Magdala, but it seemed like I was someone else, as if I was something's puppet. I did things I didn't want to do regardless of whether I wanted to do them or not. Then more spirits came in, and I was powerless to stop them. At first, my business flourished, but that came with a price. At night I convulsed, tore my clothes, heard voices and screamed at the top of my lungs. I decided to make them leave me, but if I even *spoke* about being free of them, well...."

Her voice trailed off, and for a moment I thought she was finished. "But Jesus cast them out. They'll never be in me again. Which brings up that word again. *How.*"

We walked a few steps, the mutual question heavy on our minds:

Who was this man Jesus?

Our path to the tomb meandered over several gentle hills, down a dip, then across a narrow, stone footbridge over a weed-choked ravine. The bridge was slightly damaged by the earthquake three days before, and we had to step carefully around some debris. Suddenly, what at first appeared to be a long, thick length of braided rope laying near the end of the footbridge, came alive. It hissed, then slithered towards us, raising its head and trying to bite us even as it approached. In the lamp's yellow light, I quickly recognized the snake to be a deadly horned viper, Judea's most poisonous serpent, and this was the biggest I'd ever seen.

Mary Magdalene stifled a scream, and we both took a step backward. Then I remembered what Jesus said so long ago: a piece of wood will save me. Emboldened, I stepped forward and whacked it three times with my staff. It writhed once and rolled over on its back, dead. I maneuvered it off the bridge into the weeds with my stick. Trembling, we continued on our way.

As we approached the tomb, we discussed how we were going to get the stone rolled away from the entrance, for it weighed thousands of pounds. The guards were sure to be surly after spending the entire night guarding a grave, and, unquestionably, they wouldn't exert themselves for us. Mary considered bribing them. I thought we could just explain that our culture required access to the body and unless they wanted us to go to the Sanhedrin to have the Centurion order them to guard Jesus's stinking corpse for the next several weeks, to let us in. All at once I turned my ankle on a loose cobblestone and fell. My satchel opened as it hit the ground, and bags of spices scattered about. I rubbed my foot and gathered the bags, Mary bent to help, but I waved her off. "Go on ahead. Maybe your bribe will work. We can always use the threat of them guarding a stinky tomb later." She smiled through her tears and went ahead. I could feel my ankle swelling, and my staff became my walking stick again. When I finally managed to hobble to her side, she was standing just inside the courtyard, facing the entrance of the tomb.

Several Roman military torches and a merrily burning campfire illuminated the area. To my surprise, the stone had been rolled away, the grave was open, and the guards were nowhere to be found.

Mary Magdalene was the first to find her tongue. "They have taken him away."

Taken him away? Gone? Dazed, I sat clumsily on a large, rough, chunk of rock across from the tomb and yelped when I felt a spike of white-hot pain shoot up my spine. Great. My injured ankle is twice its size, and now my back feels like it's on fire. All I needed was a swarm of bees to attack and my morning would be complete.

"His body gone? Oh no. How can this be? "I buried my face in my hands and started sobbing. The grotesque unfairness of it all came crashing down on me. On the behest of the ruling council of the Jews, the Romans had taken an innocent man—Jesus, my nephew—scourged him, flogged him, crucified him, and now someone was playing political games with his corpse.

Then, through my tears, I felt a comforting arm across my shoulders. I looked up, and Mary Magdalene was with me. We sat silently for a while.

Finally, she rose. "We must tell the disciples."

I tried to stand, but the pain from my ankle and back was too much. "Go. Run like the wind and tell them. I will wait here."

She kissed the top of my head and was off. I hobbled to a wooden bench near a pile of leaves and rubble. After checking for vipers and spiders, I tried to get comfortable. I must have fallen asleep, for after what seemed like just a few minutes, I woke to John's nimble footsteps coming up the street, followed by Peter's more cumbersome, thudding gait.

A moment later, both men ran past me to the tomb. John stood outside looking in, but Peter pushed past and entered. When they emerged, Peter's face betrayed his confusion, but John's seemed thoughtful. About that time Mary Magdalene returned, and they questioned us about what we had seen. When we told them everything, even about Cleopas's dream, they thanked us and departed.

Mary wrapped my ankle in some of the burial linen we had brought, enabling me to get around by using my staff as a crutch. Together, we slowly made our way to what was supposed to be Jesus's final resting place. Mary bent over to look in, gasped, and froze in place. I tugged on her robe, impatient to learn what had surprised her. I pushed past and stuck my face into the opening. To my amazement, two men wearing bright white robes were sitting where his body was supposed to be, one at the head, the other at the foot.

They asked her, "Woman, why are you crying?"

She sputtered, "They have taken my Lord away, and I don't know where they have put him."

I was confused. Who were these men in the tomb, and why were they there? Overwhelmed by the past three days' events, I found myself leaning against the tomb's opening, weeping uncontrollably. The blood was pounding in my ears, and I was dizzy. The world seemed to have no meaning. Then I heard Mary talking to a man behind us. Somehow his voice sounded familiar, and I turned to face them.

It was Jesus. He was alive again.

Mary ran to his side and, laughing, hugged his legs. My heart leaped for joy. Suddenly I realized my ankle and back no longer hurt. I quickly joined my friend worshiping Jesus as the Son of God. Mary and I started crying again, but this time our tears were joyful, and laughter filled our hearts.

Jesus is alive!

You may call that your own which no man can take from you.

Golden B Flat Cinnamon

Imagine being known by musical notes, color, scent, and mathematical symbols. That is how God named us angels in heaven. There are other things we are known by too, but humans won't understand until they get here.

If they get here.

There are so many angels that our creator got creative. I was named C Sharp Lime Sky Blue. I have some mathematical symbols too—the kind that Einstein dreamt about. That was my identity. Sounds silly to you humans, I am sure, but it works very well, and I like it.

I was friends with Golden B Flat Cinnamon. One day he came to me and said quietly, "There's a revolution starting up." Lucifer, the most beautiful of the angels, was planning to overthrow the Almighty. I had never, ever thought about such a thing before.

"No!" I cried. "This must never be." Then Lucifer came by and presented his plan; Initially, I admit I was curious, and we angels had free will to choose too, so...

But after a moment, I rejected what he was saying, for I could be loyal only to God.

I went to Gabriel the Archangel. "Heads up," I said. "Lucifer's plotting." Gabriel shrugged and sort of said, "It's all under control." I was a bit alarmed, and frankly, I didn't like his passivity.

I went to Michael. He said much the same thing.

Finally, I decided to approach God with my concerns. I wasn't afraid, nor was I hesitant. Jehovah is everywhere, so finding him was easy. I was sure that he knew what was going on.

"I know the future," he said.

I replied, "Yes, Father, you *are* the future. And the past. And the present. But you should know about this *now*."

He never responded. But I felt his love for me even stronger, which reassured me, for a while.

I watched as Lucifer approached all the angels in heaven—and I was alarmed when almost a third swore their allegiance to Lucifer.

I tried to reason with Golden B Flat Cinnamon. "God created us from nothing," I said. "How does the *created* have the power to rebel against the *creator*? In the barest part of one second, could God not reduce us to nothing?"

My friend leaned close to tell me something that took me off guard. He confided in me that Lucifer had looked him in the eye and guaranteed him the spot at his right hand, *the* position of power and authority—if he followed him.

I replied that our tasks here in heaven *were* positions of power and authority, but he would have none of it. He took me by my shoulders, looked deeply into my eyes, and said, "Just think. Me. At Lucifer's right hand. You will have a powerful friend in High Places. Me. I won't forget you, Sky Blue."

At once I understood. In all creation, Lucifer had utilized pride. Pride breeds envy and envy breeds contempt. But God's love is enough for us; it's all we need.

There is no squabbling or strife here in heaven. We angels each have our places; we have perfect love from God. That alone is sufficient for us. Sadly, Lucifer had become envious of God. He was the angel of music and light, and he was breathtakingly beautiful. But it wasn't enough for him.

I had an idea. Maybe I could stop the rebellion if Lucifer would listen to me—so I went to him. I was dazzled by his brilliance. And when he spoke, he didn't merely talk, but instead, he sang in the most beautiful voice I'd ever heard. I listened to him, but with the knowledge, that pride was his fuel. When he was done, he asked me to join him.

This I would not do, *could* not do, and I told him so. In his eyes, I saw disappointment and something else: bitterness.

I urged Lucifer to approach God and repent, but he shook his head. Then I saw something else: regret. "I must do what I must. This is my destiny. Join me. You will sit at my right hand."

I remembered what Golden B Flat Cinnamon had said, and I replied, "I thought you had promised that spot to another angel." Lucifer laughed, and his voice boomed across the universe. Then he leaned close and whispered, "You're a greater being than all of them. Join me. We will do great things together. We shall rule."

I shook my head. "I cannot. I will not. You are wrong, Lucifer."

At once, Lucifer turned away, and I saw another thing for the first time: rage.

When he was gone, I was devastated. There was nothing that I wanted more than to have heaven remain unchanged, but it seemed that events were about to alter it forever. But the more I wrestled with the issue, the more I yielded to and trusted God. I was confident He would prevail.

So, when Lucifer made his move against the Almighty, I watched as the Father cast him and his followers down from heaven like a bolt of lightning to earth. Sadly, Golden B Flat Cinnamon went too.

While we angels exist independent of time, we don't know the future, so I watched as history unfolded. Lucifer's name became 'Satan,' synonymous with 'liar' and 'accuser'—and I saw his beauty turned into perversion. I saw how he tricked Eve, then Adam. I saw their removal from the Garden of Eden.

I saw hatred, envy, strife, war, pestilence, death and corruption take its toll on humankind. With each passing century, I saw Satan's minions harass and torment the inhabitants of Earth.

Pure evil.

I saw the great flood with dismay but was relieved to watch the Ark with Noah's family inside float above the waters. I witnessed the prophets come and go. I read the Torah and the rest of the Old Testament. There was no end to the evil and wickedness that plagued the world. I saw mankind wrestle with malevolence on every side. I thought humanity was doomed.

Until I had my Jesus moment.

Actually, I had many. I stood with Gabriel and watched as he told Mary she was to conceive of the Holy Spirit. I had the honor of explaining the birth of a tiny baby who would be the savior of the world to Joseph, Mary's husband-to-be.

When Jesus was born, I stood above the shepherd's fire and proclaimed the birth of the savior of mankind. I saw the initial fear and confusion on their faces turn to joy as they realized what an honor that God bestowed on them. As they discussed going to see the infant, I inspired their sheep to bleat 'Go,' and I watched over their flock in their absence.

I watched Jesus grow up. I saw him make the blind see, the sick healthy, the lame walk. I saw people's hearts turn towards his.

And I watched other's hearts turn away.

I heard him speak of the love of God, his impending death on the cross, and his resurrection from the grave. I saw Jesus, during his darkest hours in the garden of Gethsemane, begging the Father to lift the cup of death from him.

I heard the Father's deafening silence.

I watched as Jesus was led away to be scourged and die an awful death on the cross for those who were alive—and those yet to be born.

I saw him conquer death and arise from the tomb.

Glorious. I saw it all. In retrospect, even though I am an angel, I can see why I thought God needed my help: my conception of God was too small.

Yesterday, I had an opportunity to speak with my former angelic friend, Golden B Flat Cinnamon. Dozens upon dozens of centuries spreading Satan's lies and doing his evil intent had changed him into a hideous shell of his former self.

"To the conqueror goes the plunder, my old friend," he said, as he held up a skull and licked it. I noticed his tongue was forked and reptilian-like. "Like it? My latest trophy. Her name isn't even important anymore. I've tricked so many."

"Tricked?"

"Euthanasia of the elderly, my specialty. Make them think life is not worth living anymore. I introduce pain, sprinkle in a bit of confusion, and they die without knowing God."

I noted that my friend spoke without enthusiasm, and he continued, "Little do they know that all they have to do is repent and accept Jesus's salvation. Then they will spend eternity with Jesus." His voice trailed off. "I used to have eternity with God. What a stupid thing I did by listening to Satan."

"The Bible says your time is short, Golden B Flat Cinnamon. Can you still repent and be welcomed back into heaven? Would you like me to ask Jesus for you?"

"No, my friend. And, my name changed after the fall. I am known as 'Rot' now. We all are. I should have stayed in heaven with you. Not a day goes by that I don't regret my choice. I'm compelled to do Satan's will now, but..."

I had to get away. "Help your next victim, Rot. Here is a chance for you to do good. Resist your evil nature, friend. Fight it."

He shrugged as I was leaving, but I thought I heard him say quietly, "I will try."

I returned to heaven and sought the Father for mercy on my friend. I felt his loving kindness flood through my being, and once again I accepted the endless choice we made so long ago. We angels are destined to stay in heaven with God or be cast into the lake of fire at the end of days for following Lucifer.

The Father showed me Rot talking to an elderly man in a nursing home. The man was a highly-decorated war hero, some 94 years of age. His wife, his children, and all his friends had already passed. The man, sitting in his easy chair, was clutching a worn Bible in his trembling hands. His wife had read it for many years, but despite her prayers for him, long ago battles had hardened the old soldier's heart, and he thought himself unworthy of God's forgiveness. Tears flowed down his weathered face. On the floor was a crumbled-up brochure from a euthanasia firm. A Silver Star medal for heroism in combat lay near.

Then something amazing happened. Rot opened the Bible to the book of John, chapter three, verse sixteen; with shaking talons, he lifted the man's finger to caress the passage. He smiled at Rot, for his vision was dim and his time was very near. Together they read aloud, "For God so loved the world that he gave his one and only son, that whoever believes in him shall not perish, but have eternal life."

Rot explained the significance of the verse and looked away. I could see the muscles in Rot's back stand out like cables. Tendrils of neon-red sulfur gas started to seep out of his nostrils, and his body shook as he fought the titanic struggle to suppress his evil nature.

I cheered him on.

Then suddenly evil won, and he roared at the man, "No.

You cannot believe this, sergeant. You must not. Remember the caves of Iwo Jima? The beach at Tarawa? Chosin Reservoir? You have killed men in horrible ways. You cannot be forgiven. It's a lie."

The old warrior's back stiffened as if he were at attention on the military parade ground.

Then he fought his final battle.

In a voice much younger than his years, the sergeant shouted back, "No, it's not a lie. You're wrong. Not believing is a lie. This verse is the truth, and yes, I do believe it now, with all my heart. I am not a monster, I never was. You are." With his last bit of strength, the sergeant pushed the demon away. Then he slumped in his chair and was no more.

Pure evil again, Rot raked the air in front of the man's body with his talons as he ran around the room, shrieking, "No no no no no you must not—" before vanishing.

All the angels rejoiced as the hero's soul entered heaven, welcomed by his wife, friends, and family. I cheered the loudest, and the longest, for I had seen my friend do something extraordinary. Sadly, Golden B Flat Cinnamon's fate was sealed when he elected to follow Lucifer, but somehow, as the demon 'Rot', he led that man to victory in Christ rather than an eternity of misery away from God. I rejoiced even more.

I said to the Father, "Thank you for allowing my friend to help that old soldier. Thank you." I felt His loving kindness wash over my being for a very long time.

As it ebbed, the Almighty shrugged and said, "Fuhgeddaboudit."

The End

We can easily forgive a child who is afraid of the dark.
The real tragedy of life is when men are afraid of the Light.

Acknowledgements

A hearty 'thank you' goes out to my wife and children for their undying love, patience, and support. Thanks too, to David Casper (DavidCasperMusic. com) for his help navigating the nuances of Latin.

A special 'thank you' needs to go to my editors, Janey DeMeo of Orphans First ministries (OrphansFirst.org) and Suzanne Gleason. Thanks too, to my gifted illustrator, Heather Miller, and the genius of design, Jesica Rogus, for her work on the front and back covers.

A resounding 'thank you' to my friends Lee Rizio and David Burris for their painstaking commentary and boundless enthusiasm on this project.

Below each story is a quote taken from 'Apples of Gold,' a compilation of wisdom by Jo Petty, and published in 1962 by The C.R. Gibson Company of Norwalk, Connecticut. In the forward of her book, Jo writes, "The material in this book has been collected over a long period of time. Many of the original sources are unknown to the compiler. The compiler wishes to acknowledge the original authors, whoever they may be, but has confidence that they would urge, with her, "Do not inquire as to who said this, but pay attention to what is said."

Keep in mind this is a work of fiction. I've taken some literary license, and I hope you've enjoyed my efforts.

Last—but never least—God gets my praise, and He deserves yours too.

Stone Thrower is available in softcover and Kindle (e-book) format on Amazon.com and Barnes&Noble BN.com.

Oh, one more thing: please leave an honest review on either—or both—sites.

Mike Casper

Also by Mike Casper

An unlikely love story, set in medieval times but relevant for today.

Available in *paperback* and *Kindle* (e-book) on Amazon.com and Barnes&Noble BN.com

About the Author

Mike Casper is a Southern California author with a gift and a passion for storytelling. He is a world traveler, a husband, a father, and is an avid reader with varied life experiences. Mike believes although life can be tragic, it can also be beautiful.

Mike also thinks that books will take you to places that no other media can, and with that in mind, he wrote STONE THROWER and THE SING SONG CHILD.

Enjoy the journey.

67628722R00090

Made in the USA
Columbia, SC
02 August 2019